Praise for Lauren Fox's

Send for Me

"Imbued with lyrical prose, *Send for Me* is a beautiful tale of heartbreak and renewal, and of the love and loss we carry with us, generation after generation."
—Georgia Hunter, author of *We Were the Lucky Ones*

"Page after page of *Send for Me* shines with the author's brilliant prose. . . . Fox has written a book you will not soon forget." —*The Florida Times-Union*

"*Send for Me* is a rare and beautiful novel. . . . I loved this book."
—Christina Baker Kline, author of *Orphan Train*

"Resonates long after its final pages. . . . Its beautifully rendered vignettes are, in essence, about 'the fraying wire' that connects us to the past." —*The Anniston Star* (Alabama)

"Extraordinarily nuanced and moving. . . . Fox elegantly incorporates lines and short excerpts of her own great-grandmother's letters, adding to the power and intimacy of this fine novel." —*The National Book Review*

"Subtle, striking, and punctuated by snippets of family letters. . . . An intimate, insightful, intricately rendered story of intergenerational trauma and love."
—*Kirkus Reviews* (starred review)

Lauren Fox

Send for Me

Lauren Fox is the author of the novels *Days of Awe*, *Still Life with Husband*, and *Friends Like Us*. Her work has appeared in *The New York Times*, *The Wall Street Journal*, *Marie Claire*, *Parenting*, and *Psychology Today*. She lives in Milwaukee with her family.

Send for Me

Send for Me

LAUREN FOX

VINTAGE BOOKS

A DIVISION OF PENGUIN RANDOM HOUSE LLC

NEW YORK

The Library of Congress has cataloged
the Knopf edition as follows:
Names: Fox, Lauren, author.
Title: Send for me / Lauren Fox.
Description: First edition. |
New York : Alfred A. Knopf, 2021.
Identifiers: LCCN 2020017934 (print) |
LCCN 2020017935 (ebook)
Subjects: GSAFD: Historical fiction. | Love stories.
Classification: LCC PS3606.095536 S46 2021 (print) |
LCC PS3606.095536 (ebook) | DDC 813/.6—dc23
LC record available at https://lccn.loc.gov/2020017934
LC ebook record available
at https://lccn.loc.gov/2020017935

Vintage Books Trade Paperback ISBN: 978-1-101-97204-5
eBook ISBN: 978-1-101-94781-4

www.vintagebooks.com

Printed in the United States of America
10 9 8 7 6 5 4 3 2 1

For my parents

and my daughters

Section One

I can hardly speak.

It starts with the panic, the sound of sharp knocking. The pounding on Annelise's door, a crash in her skull, jolting her from sleep. *They're coming.* Her heart slams, and she sits up, blind in the darkness. Her arms reach out. *Where is the baby?* Fear floods her lungs. She's drowning.

They're coming. Breathe. Hold the baby close, keep her quiet.

Is there something else in the churning flood of terror? In the squeeze of panic, the slightest slackening, relief? She's been waiting so long for this moment, dread her constant companion, and now it's here. Whatever horror is about to befall her, she won't have to fear it any longer.

In the room, silent now, she strains to hear. Her heart is pounding so hard her body is thrumming, her hands trembling. Is that her husband next to her, snoring softly? Is that the warm, reassuring shape of him? They will take him, too. They'll take all of it, everything and everyone she has ever loved. In an instant. A flash.

Years will pass, a long, surprising slant of light, and this terror will abate. She will pick her daughter up from school, stand in her kitchen with her hands on her hips, sip from a glass in the evening, slip under smooth sheets. But this will always be her frozen moment, the definition of her days. They will always be pounding on the door in the middle of the night. They will always be coming.

An hour doesn't pass that I don't think about you.

There is so much work to do. Toil is a constant in her life, the ongoing story of her years. In fact, Klara takes some comfort in its predictability, the way that a Sunday afternoon of polishing silver or washing floors can ease her nerves and stretch her mind into a pleasant blankness. And there is the undeniable satisfaction of a task completed, the pleasing order and gleam of a finely tended home.

Of course, there's also the bakery: her pride and livelihood, yes, but oh, those dreadful dark mornings, the midday heat, the relentless specifics of the measurements, the unforgiving timing of every little thing. Some days she wakes up, dawn still hours away, and the exhaustion of the day before clings to her; she would want to roll over and go back to sleep if she allowed herself even to want that.

Klara can never let on, can never show this weakness. Annelise grouses and mutters and yawns dramatically, stares with sullen dark eyes and refuses to speak for hours, the spectacle of her displeasure so varied and colorful, she's like a peacock of disdain.

She envies her daughter's extravagance. But Klara can't allow herself to crack. A word of complaint from her could loose an avalanche.

The precision of the bakery does, in a way, appeal to her

nature, but it's such a precarious balance. They can't make any mistakes or they pay double, triple the price in lost revenue.

It changes a person—all of it, the tasks at hand. Klara has changed—of course she has! She's become someone who is entirely focused on the work she must do. But that's simply what it is to be a woman of good standing, to be alive in the world. It defies consideration.

Early in her marriage, there were mishaps: the loaf of bread that almost burned down the apartment, the boiled egg, forgotten, that exploded in the kitchen, sending bits of shell like shrapnel flying around the room. She cleaned up every last splinter before Annelise woke, before Julius came into the kitchen for coffee, and so only Klara herself, who accidentally knelt on a sharp chip of eggshell, was even slightly injured. She considers that injury . . . what? Not a punishment, exactly, but a reminder, the quick, searing pain a covenant. She learned not to make those mistakes, and in learning, she has become intolerant of laxity. And so, she has become intolerant of her own daughter.

How did such a girl come from her? Annelise was such an industrious child when she was small, so cheerful and competent, her dear little helper! But now she's almost fifteen, and a fog has settled over her. Now Annelise is alternately dreamy and resentful, her work at the bakery halfhearted at best. She suffers no remorse when she leaves a domestic task half done, when (sighing) she mops around the kitchen table instead of underneath it, when she takes the feather duster to the living room and then, halfway through, for no apparent reason, simply abandons her task.

Yes, Klara adores her daughter, of course she does. It's just that it is so much easier to adore her after the work is done. But this is the problem: the work is never done. And so, when Annelise complains—or when she mumbles under her breath, or dallies, or says, "I'll do it in just a few minutes," frustration blooms in Klara like deadly nightshade.

There was the warm Tuesday evening, just last week, when Klara dragged herself home after a long day at the bakery (poor, dependable Julius was still there, finishing the orders, closing the store). Klara trudged up the apartment stairs, expertly finessed the stubborn lock and opened the door to their apartment, and walked into an unholy, godforsaken mess: breakfast dishes still on the table (not even soaking in the sink), Annelise's books and papers strewn about the living room, her cello propped against the wall, dressing gown on the floor like a puddle of pink cotton, an apple core on the piano. And there: Annelise herself, draped across the sofa, face slack and peaceful, asleep. Asleep!

Well. A flame ignited inside Klara; she could almost hear the pop. She had been at the bakery since four in the morning. Her ankles were swollen, her feet practically screaming out loud with pain. She was coated in sugar and flour and oil and sweat, a slick organic grime. She had asked Annelise to start dinner, to boil the potatoes and peel the carrots, but there was no sign of any work having been done. My God, she was bone-weary, and now this: *hours* ahead of her.

Klara, electrified with fury, shook her daughter awake. "What is the matter with you?" she barked. "Get up! *Get up!*" She was wild, murderous. She shook Annelise's shoulders harder than necessary, allowed her fingers the momentary pleasure of digging roughly into her daughter's flesh.

"Mama!" Annelise's voice was high and choked. She had been ripped from a lovely, dozy dream: she was performing a cello recital, every note perfection. For the briefest moment her mother's scolding overlapped with Tchaikovsky's Nocturne. Annelise blinked, registered the bite of Klara's fingers into her shoulders, her mother's blotchy-pink, enraged face hovering above hers. Her eyes watered. "I'm sorry," she squeaked. "I fell asleep."

"Obviously," Klara hissed. "Clean up this mess right now!" She turned on her heels and headed into the kitchen to begin her next shift. From the living room, Annelise's sobs were tiny, gulping chirps. A second ago, Klara had been so mad she'd been quaking. But just as suddenly as it had combusted, the flame was doused. A liquid embarrassment seeped through her edges now. She was still wearing her shoes, her cloth coat, but she couldn't go back into the living room to put them away. She blinked back her own tears as she attacked the potatoes with the sharp peeling knife.

She was training Annelise to function without her. That's what she was doing. One doesn't always remember it in the busy slog of the day, but that is the project. A mother teaches her daughter to perpetuate the tedious rituals of her own imperfect life. And by instilling in her child the virtues of order, she shows her how to keep the chaos at bay. It's not always pleasant. But what else is there?

But in a dark house, at night, next to her sleeping husband, she aches for the moments she didn't touch Annelise as she passed, the times she didn't praise her beautiful cello playing; how easy it would be to whisper to her what she is, *my treasure,* to kiss her dark head. Regret is a low, constant throb.

Klara shrugged off her coat, draped it over a kitchen chair, and began stripping the potatoes with an expert *fwip-fwip.* The kitchen grew dim as evening settled. She peeled and peeled. Potatoes accumulated in the pot like white stones in cold water. The apartment was quiet, and, after a long time, she was calm.

Now I have several questions to ask you, Annelise. I went through some of your things yesterday and I saw that your curtains were here. You'll need these right away. Shall I put them aside? What about the rose-colored dress with the matching coat and the black coat? Red sweater? Black dress that we bought in Frankfurt? Answer all of these questions, please.

Annelise trudges into the bakery with her parents every morning before sunrise, bleary and taciturn. The predawn darkness is so deeply at odds with her body's clock that she sometimes feels as if she's sleepwalking, still mid-dream. As her parents bicker about who forgot to order more white sugar or sweep the front step, she twists her hair into a bun and ties her white apron around her waist. The black coffee she drank before she left the house will spark her senses soon. On her mother's strict orders, she'll put on her cheeriest face for the customers. Mohnkuchen? Pfeffernüsse? Streuselkuchen? This is her job, although of course she doesn't get paid. It's the family business, so it's her duty, her burden, and, she has no reason to doubt, her inheritance.

She finished school at the Gymnasium in the spring, just three months ago, and although she was never a brilliant student, she feels the loss of that part of her life acutely now, sharp as a pencil tip. She misses the daily chats with Emmi and Sofie, the pleasure of mastering her subjects, the smell of chalk and polished floors, the forward motion. Now, it's Bäckerei Adler that gives shape to her hours, and the only way out is marriage and children—and even then, she'll likely be pressed back into service sooner rather than later, when her theoretical children are old enough to go to school. She'll untie this white apron and exchange it for a different one, and then, in a few years, she'll knot herself back into this one. Her life unfurls before her, apron after apron.

She pulls the rag bucket from under the sink and takes out a clean cloth (a scrap of an old apron, as a matter of fact), soaks it in vinegar and water, and begins to scrub down the counter. Her parents are in the back, beginning the day's baking, companionable now in their predictable rhythms. The smell of yeast hits her nostrils first; then, depending on the day, next will be cinnamon or ginger or, her favorite, anise, bright and slightly bitter.

What is it that she wants? A different burden of responsibilities? A passion she can't define? Simple escape? She loves to read, she likes to draw, she is a reasonably accomplished cellist. But so what? She blows a stray wisp of hair out of her eyes, attacks a smudge on the glass with excessive vigor. She just knows: not this. Her discontent is undefined, undefinable, and so the bakery has become its focus. She hates the relentless, dull routine, the heat, the dirty utensils forever needing to be washed. She despises it with a contempt that will, after everything that comes later, reconfigure itself into a hot and stunning shame.

Outside, she hears the first clanks and clatters of Feldenheim rattling to life. The sun is coming up now, dim glow edging through the storefront window. Midday, it will be so bright and hot in here that Annelise will have to crank the awning, but for now, this light is gentle and perfect.

There are some tolerable things about the bakery, if she's honest with herself. For example, she is no great beauty— she knows this. She's short, a little too curvy. Her eyes are as brown as a mud puddle, and her hair is impossible. But behind the glass bakery counter, she is in her element, a sea creature, an exotic, dark-haired mermaid swimming in a sea of crusty breads and sugar-dusted pastries. The scent of rising yeast lingers in the air, intoxicating. Young men on their way to class place their orders, brötchen, a slice of apfelkuchen or streusel, and smile at her hungrily. On occasional, quiet moments throughout the long day, she imagines herself irresistible.

Max Eisenberg, student of art history, friend of her youth, stops in nearly every day for pflaumenkuchen, which her mother bakes especially for him. When it's still warm, Annelise will cut a generous slice, arrange it on a plate, and set it aside for him. These days, she mitigates the tedium by thinking ahead to his visit, how he will walk in at some point during the lull between the 8:30 rush and the 12:00 chaos, grinning at her, waiting patiently if there are people ahead of him.

She imagines his familiar smile and the new thrill of it. She and Max grew up together, their families neighbors in adjoining apartments. His mother and hers were as close as sisters, and Max and Annelise were born only a few weeks apart—Annelise first, in the middle of dreary February, and then Max, during the first soft lick of spring. They had been raised, until they were ten, as if their mothers were interchangeable. When they were very young, Klara and Dora fed them together, bathed them together, and often, after the children had played for hours, tucked them into the same bed. Annelise knew Max—the sharp jut of his elbows, the little gap between his front teeth, the grassy smell of his skin; the way he stood at the edge of a crowd, too shy to participate until she dragged him in; how, the winter they turned nine, he taught himself to speak in burps and wished her a happy birthday in loud, musical belches.

In the summer of 1922, the year they were ten, Max's father, Karl, who drank too much and sometimes hit Dora, left.

"Good riddance," Annelise's parents said; "good riddance," Dora echoed, with a quavery catch in her voice. In Annelise's memory, that was all they said, a constant refrain, but she knew that Max cried himself to sleep. A few months later, Max and Dora moved into a smaller apartment a few miles away, in an older, less prosperous part of the city. The distance cost their friendship nothing. He was her brother.

Which is why their first kiss, three weeks ago, shortly after Annelise began working full-time at the bakery and Max started classes at the university, was a shock to both of them. They came together practically by accident—*was* it an accident?—in the cluttered kitchen of Max's mother's apartment, and then both jumped back as if their lips repelled each other, the north-seeking poles of two magnets. But it was just as shocking how quickly they came back together, seconds later, eager and undeterred, how their familiarity recalibrated and became a sparkling curiosity.

"Lise?" Max whispered, as if he weren't quite sure who she was. She felt the sharp corner of the counter poke into her back. Max's hand, in a confused flutter, patted her head, then came to rest on her shoulder. *What is this?* she thought, and then, *Why not?* It was the best kiss of her life. It was the only kiss of her life.

Ever since then, they've been sneaking around like teenagers, which they are: back in his apartment, while his mother is out shopping; in the bakery, after her parents have gone home, when she is supposed to be sweeping the floors and double-checking to be sure the ovens are cool and the lights are off. Their lives are enmeshed, but her options are limited, which makes their moments together more thrilling. Max wraps his arms around his old friend and whispers his plans to her—*after university . . . the two of us . . . Berlin.*

All they've done is kiss. Is there more than that? She's eighteen years old, and she's quite sure there is. She and Emmi and Sofie used to whisper about boys they liked, but those boys were abstractions: blue eyes, quick learners; jokesters or thinkers, fast runners or quiet readers; unknowable hearts.

Now, with Max, her oldest friend, she's in a constant, heightened state, whirring like the bakery's cast-iron hand mixer. She is waking up, wanting. The haze inside her is being burned away by the unlikeliest of kindling. In between carefully monitoring rising dough and wrapping loaves of bread for customers, Annelise is beginning to reimagine her future.

He stops in after his classes, his leather book bag slung over his shoulder. Klara peers around the corner as soon as she hears his voice. Her round face is bright pink from the heat of the industrial ovens. "You're coming for dinner tonight, darling," she tells him, clapping her hands together, sending up a little puff of flour, and Max says, "Yes, thanks," and when Klara hustles back to her work area, Max grins at Annelise, and they share this buzzing secret, and the electricity of it carries her through the rest of her long day.

*

They sit across from each other at the dining room table, curtains open to the fading light of the day. Max teases Annelise for having flour in her hair, and he fights her for the last potato, finally spearing it with his fork and waving it at her. Klara asks him about his classes, and Julius is his typical quiet self, nodding in peaceable agreement, letting his wife speak for him, but he likes to make up nicknames for the customers at the bakery, and today he tells Klara and Max and Annelise about his favorites: Willi the Walrus, the man whose mustache curled low beneath his droopy face, and Mother Goose, the woman who kept her four tiny, blond children in a straight line behind her at all times. Annelise snorts when she laughs, and Max kicks her under the table, and they're just like they've always been: practically siblings. But then, after dinner, after eating the anise cookies she baked this afternoon, while her mother is doing the dishes, Annelise walks Max out, and he kisses her in the stairwell, the taste of licorice still on their tongues, and she runs, flushed, back to her apartment.

One day, a few weeks into this—what is it? they've never actually said—Max doesn't show up at the bakery, not at all. At six in the evening, Annelise, not exactly worried but not exactly *not* worried, folds up her apron and untwists her hair and sweeps and scrubs and locks the door with the feeling that fourteen empty hours have just sifted through her fingers.

He doesn't come in the next day, either, and so, late in the afternoon, when the store is quiet and the bread is sold and all that's left are a few slices of streuselkuchen and a couple of kipferln, Annelise slips away and walks quickly to the café where they sometimes meet, her heels clopping hard on the narrow cobblestone sidewalk. The café is seven long blocks from the bakery, and when she arrives she's breathing heavily and perspiring, even though the day is cool. She pushes the heavy door open and sees him almost immediately, sitting alone at a round table near the window, a cigarette burning in an ashtray, his books and notebooks spread out in front of him. She stands there for a second, in the doorway, wiping her sweaty hands down the sides of her green dress, blocking foot traffic until someone pushes past her and she is forced to come all the way in. Max, sensing the movement, looks up and sees her.

Annelise is, to her surprise, overcome with anger. *Where have you been?* she wants to say. *Where the hell have you been?* She is crackling with rage, a fishwife, a shrew. But she's eighteen years old. She is not that. She raises a palm to her warm face, feels suddenly like crying. She swallows, walks over to him, trying to be casual, knowing instinctively that her approach to this situation is important.

"I was just feeling a little hungry," she says brightly. "So I thought I'd stop in for a pastry. Didn't know where else to go around here!"

Max laughs, puts his book down, and pats the chair next to him. "I'm sorry," he says, and Annelise sits and tries to gauge the warmth in his tone from those two words. He moves his hand in a circle over the smooth grain of the table. "I had to study," he says. She leans in close to hear him over the din of the café. He juts his chin toward the books and papers. "I have so much work to do."

She nods, startled by how the slightest change in Max's gaze, the dip of his head, the flicker of his focus, transforms her. Two days ago, she was a perfect composition of face and limbs and breath and heart. Now she is a rag doll, lumpy, mismatched, stitched together and stuffed with old cloth.

Max's hand is resting, fingers splayed, palm down, on the table, and Annelise moves her own hand toward his at the exact moment that he reaches for his cigarette, and they do not touch: an awkward ballet.

I love you, she thinks. *I love you, I love you, I love you.* She is not stupid enough to say this out loud, but she feels her face go soft, her eyes watery with an ocean of affection, and Annelise hopes that Max is too preoccupied to notice.

This moment is nothing, really. Her heart will mend: Even as she can practically feel it cracking, she has an inkling that it will eventually glue itself back together. Maybe it's even starting right now, the delicate process of repair. This is not a devastation like the ones that will follow, nothing like those great, gasping, winged monsters of ruin that will come later, the ones that will try to pick her up in their claws and fling her to her death. It's nothing like those, obviously, but still, years from now, in another country with her handsome husband, this life irrevocably behind her, she will remember it: the smell of coffee beans and cigarette smoke, the clink of dishes and the laughter drifting over from other tables, the sudden rearrangement of their relationship reflected in Max's face.

Her life will not unfold in any way she can possibly imagine in this nothing-moment: neither gently, with an abundance of love, nor roughly, under the pressing weight of obligation.

One week later, Max does come into the bakery, and Annelise looks up from the table she's cleaning and feels as if she's being lifted into the air and dropped suddenly. A little gasp, the softest *oh*, escapes her mouth.

Max—of course, of course—is holding the door for a tall woman who looks like a lioness, sharp, fine features and reddish hair and green eyes gazing around like she's deciding which small mammal she will eat. Max catches Annelise's eye. They head toward her. Annelise will not be the small mammal! She straightens, tucks her cleaning rag into her apron pocket, smooths a strand of hair that has escaped its tie, but anyone can see it's too late for all of that.

"This is Katarina," Max says, and Katarina nods at Annelise, offers her hand to shake. "She's studying cartography at the university." He turns to Katarina. "And this is Lise," he says. "My oldest friend."

Fifty years later Annelise will sit at a long wooden table, an enormous book in front of her, and she will slide her glasses down her nose and trace her finger down a column of tiny print and she'll find their names: Max Eisenberg, 32, Auschwitz; Katarina Eisenberg, 33, Auschwitz; Otto Eisenberg, 7, Auschwitz. She will want to slam the book shut, but this book is too heavy to slam, and so, instead, she will just close it, very carefully, until, a minute later, she'll open it again, to search for other names, which she will also find.

I've burned a lot of things on the stove this morning. It's very empty here now. There's no need for us to wait for anyone anymore on Saturdays. I need to keep busy so I can forget.

If Julius could have placed an order, all those years ago, would he have put in for a boy? Well, what man doesn't wish for a son to carry on his legacy? He imagined reading quietly with his son on a Sunday morning, playing chess with him while Klara made dinner. There would be a calm and unspoken understanding between them, two comrades against the floral-scented, overly talkative world of women.

But he fell in love with Annelise the moment the nurse placed her in his arms. Of course he did. She stared up at his face, taking its measure, blinking a secret code. He fell into an ocean of love.

Still, raising a daughter is the job of the mother, and even more so as she grows up. On more than one occasion, Julius overheard an argument between Klara and Annelise and thought, *Thank goodness I'm not a part of that!* And once in a while, from behind his newspaper, he allowed himself to dream of a boy, dark as Annelise, but quiet, uncomplicated. "Son, let's go outside and kick the ball around while those two cool off, shall we?" But they lived in an apartment on a busy street. And Julius was never any good at sport.

He envied their passion, sometimes. It was dark, crimson. It blazed between them, love and hurt, adoration and tears.

They each came to him for comfort, and he knew how to soothe them, how to put out their fires. "Klara, she's just a girl.

She's not forgetful on purpose. It's her nature. Be patient."
"Lise, dry your tears, give her time to cool off. She expects so
much from you because she loves you."

When Annelise was small, they would walk together on Sunday mornings, slow rambles to the park, where Lise would
investigate everything that caught her eye. Some days,
immersed in the path of a bee or the crunch of leaf piles, they
wouldn't make it to the park at all.

Can we catch a squirrel? Can you teach me how to cook it? ("We
don't cook squirrels," he told her. She squinted up at him, per-
plexed. "But we do cook fish?")

There was something unusual about her, her strange, curi-
ous, reckoning mind, or maybe there was something unusual
about all five-year-old little girls if you listened to them.

An image of his little brother sometimes superimposed
itself upon his daughter—Paul's green eyes replacing Lise's
brown ones, his short brown hair fading into her dark curls.
He would have to catch his breath when that happened, close
his eyes, pry the images apart.

*How do I know we see the same blue? Are teeth little bones? When
is the end of never?* She had an imaginary friend called Pillow, a
small, anxious man who needed frequent reassurance. *Don't
worry about camels, Kissen. There are no camels where we live.*

When Max broke her heart—did they think he didn't
know?—she wept in her mother's arms. Julius paced the apartment. Behind her bedroom door, Lise's sobs were melody, her

mother's low shushes the counterpoint. He had never been more useless. He walked around the living room, into the dining room, the kitchen, through the hallway, circled back again. His leather house slippers wore a path in the soft carpets.

He would march over to the apartment where Max and Dora lived, confront the damn fool. He'd stand inches from him, glowering. *You are a son of a bitch! (Apologies, dear Dora.) But what the hell do you think you're doing? How dare you* . . . Here Julius's fantasy stuttered. *How dare you decide you're not in love with my daughter?* What then, a sharp jab to the jaw? Max might be feckless, but Julius held no sway over the private matters of Annelise's heart. He wanted to slam his fist into the wall. But what would that solve? And who would fix the hole? Should he lift her up and place her feet on his and dance her around the apartment? His best ideas were futilities, all his old tricks worse than useless.

He was an observer of details. How she studied the ground after it rained, searching for worms. The neat white part down her scalp dividing her pigtails. The way she pushed beans around her plate, rearranging them as if that would fool her mother into thinking she'd eaten a few. Surly for the first hour after she woke up, loquacious before bed. It was his vocation to perceive and remember, and he did; he remembered everything. Her bitten nails. How she held a water glass with both hands. The way she paused before she spoke, as if she were slowly pulling herself out of a dream.

As soon as I get the confirmation, we will pack.

Annelise wakes up to the clang of her alarm clock on the morning of her nineteenth birthday. It's 4:00 a.m. Frost veils her bedroom window. The moon scrapes the black sky like a little chip of glass.

Misery. What would it feel like to wake up well rested, in a room bright with sunshine? She groans as she remembers that she used the last of the coffee yesterday and forgot to pick up more. She has no one to take her to the movies tonight (well, maybe Emmi, but definitely not Sofie, who is nestled cozily in her new life now and never goes out) and anyway she's too tired to go to the movies because she has to wake up every day at 4:00 a.m. And today, of all days, with no coffee. Her bed is so warm. The floor is freezing. It's Friday. It is Friday, February 13, 1931, and Annelise is miserable because she is miserable.

And what, anyway, is the pleasure of celebrating your birthday in a bakery? They are the ones who provide the sweetness for other people. As Julius likes to cheerfully announce at the table on nights when there is no after-dinner cake, nothing left over from the store, *The shoemaker's children go barefoot!*

Annelise washes up, squeezes a blob of Biox Ultra onto her toothbrush, and attacks her teeth with all of her repressed ire. She yanks the knots out of her hair and pins it up, dusts herself with talcum (feeling, as she does every morning as the sweet powder settles over her, just a little bit like a pastry herself). She gets dressed as fast as she can, rolls heavy wool socks over her frozen feet. She's ready at 4:10. She grumbles into the kitchen and puts on a pot of tea. Her parents are talking softly behind their bedroom door, her mother's alto and her father's bass, the most familiar refrain. Annelise catches herself almost smiling, and then squashes it. Will they even remember that it's her birthday?

Four months ago, on Emmi's birthday, a perfect, warm Sunday in October, the girls packed a picnic and spent the afternoon in the park. Even Sofie managed to get away for an hour. Emmi showed off the beautiful green and blue silk scarf her boyfriend had given her, and they munched on thick slices of buttered bread, boiled eggs, and squares of chocolate, until Sofie stood up, brushed crumbs off of her skirt, and declared, "Oh, girls, if I don't get home and start dinner now, Martin will starve!"

She was halfway across the park, still waving, when Emmi grabbed Annelise's arm. "Oh, no!" she said, her eyebrows furrowed.

"What is it?"

"It's just . . ." Emmi looked at Annelise, then down at the picnic blanket. "I'm afraid Martin will *starve!*"

Annelise fell back onto the blanket, giggling. "No, not dear Martin!"

Now Emmi is engaged to be married, and Annelise is sitting at the kitchen table, cradling a cup of tea still too hot to drink at 4:15 a.m. on her (most likely forgotten!) birthday, pulsing with the exquisite pain of being ripe and unpicked.

She thinks, briefly, fleetingly, about Max, as she blows on her tea and watches the steam rise. His birthday and hers were linked for so many years. For months after Max ended things, she thought she saw him everywhere: on the street, on her usual route home from the bakery, choosing fruit at the market, strolling through the park, hand in hand with a tall, reddish-haired woman. But it was never Max (knowing him, he had adopted entirely new routes), and eventually her heart stopped ramming against her rib cage every time she mistook someone else for him, and then, in time, she stopped conjuring him. But she still thinks about him, or, more accurately, she thinks about his absence, the holes in her life where he used to be.

Her parents emerge from their bedroom. Her father pulls out a chair, and her mother veers around the kitchen table and heads straight for the stove, just like always, cracking eggs and frying last night's potatoes in a pan before Annelise has swallowed two sips of her tea.

Her father looks her in the eye, smiles. *Finally!*

She looks back at him, expectant.

"Annelise."

She nods.

"You forgot to buy coffee yesterday. Would you pick some up this afternoon?"

She is nineteen years old, an adult. Her eyes fill with tears. "Of course," she says. "I'm so sorry."

"Julius!" her mother says, and her father laughs.

"Happy birthday, my dear," he says, and he passes a package across the table to her.

"Oh!" she says. It's very small, irregularly shaped, wrapped in brown paper. "What is it?"

Her mother sets a plate of eggs in front of her. "Come, let's move along," she says. "It's almost time to go." Then, the unexpected warmth of her mother's body behind her as she leans down and kisses Annelise on the head.

Annelise tucks her finger underneath the folded paper and feels the sharp poke of a small object as it slides out into her palm—a starfish brooch, silver, filigreed, with two little turquoise eyes in the middle. Its five starfish arms are plump and curved and lively, almost as if they are waving; they taper into small bejeweled tips. It's the most beautiful thing she's ever seen. She runs her fingertip over its delicate surface and has the strange urge to put it in her mouth, to suck on it; she can almost taste the cold, metallic tang.

"Thank you!" she says over the clink of dishes, the scraping of the heavy cast-iron pan. "It's beautiful."

"Your mother chose it," Julius says, and Annelise nods, but she doesn't believe him. He is the one with the eye for beauty. He's the kindest man she'll ever know, Annelise thinks. She turns to thank her mother, but she's already somewhere else. The kitchen is spotless.

Klara is hurrying through the apartment, heart thrumming with early-morning disquiet—if they don't leave in the next five minutes, their entire day at the bakery will be a rush to catch up. She's putting books away, straightening cushions, eyes on the messes that nobody else seems to notice. She bustles into Annelise's bedroom and pulls her rumpled sheets up, runs her hand over the duvet to smooth out the wrinkles. She feels the last of the remaining warmth from her daughter's sleeping body caught in the covers—the echo of her peaceful slumber, her heat.

There was something buoyant about that starfish brooch that Julius picked out for Annelise, some bright essence of their daughter. Klara recognized it immediately when he showed it to her. "It's perfect," she said to her husband. He, of course, already knew.

What love she feels for this girl, trapped in the details of this hurried, predictable, dark February morning.

In spite of everything I would not wish that you were here.

Annelise, on her bicycle, hair blowing behind her like a sail.

Or in the kitchen, alone, on a Saturday night, sipping honey-eyed tea, the stillness warm around her shoulders.

Or at the bakery, in the quiet after the first early-morning rush and just before she notices that she's hungry: her father hands her a warm brötchen on a plain white plate. It's not one of the half-ruined rolls they set aside for the family—too pale or too dense, or slightly burnt or misshapen. This one is perfect, the crust golden and hard like a shell, the bread open and airy, steam whispering away from it. And her father is smiling at her, as he hands her the warm plate, as if she is just as perfect.

Or, of course, playing a piece she knows by heart, Bach's Prelude No. 1 or the Brahms Sonata in E Minor: the music dark and low in the body of the cello, the bow an extension of her arm, her thoughts floating above her.

These are the secrets of her body, some winnowed essence of the life she is living: these fleeting moments when she is exactly where she belongs, exactly the girl she is supposed to be. Where does it come from, this brief collision of breath and astonishment? Is elation exponential, does it multiply and circle and alight on everyone, sooner or later? Is it possible that she is not the only one? Does everyone else, on occasion, take flight?

I have sold the sofa and the wardrobe in your room. Please write to me and tell me what else I should sell and what I should keep. Earlier I could buy and sell things the way I wanted to. Now I can't. Now my hand gets slapped.

If everything goes on the way it is now in Stuttgart we will still be here two years from now.

You have no idea how much I worry.

Julius knows he is tenderhearted. He comes from a long line of tenderhearted men: fathers who cry when they hold their babies for the first time, who tiptoe into darkened bedrooms just to touch the soft cheeks of their sleeping children; husbands who, at times, are filled with so much lighthearted gratitude and affection for their tired and faithful wives that they will, without suppression or regret, pull those surprised wives into their arms and hold them for a moment. Sternness is not in his nature, discipline is not his forte. He has never tried to be something he is not.

But a man keeps his own counsel. Klara long ago gave up on her youthful attempts to draw him out, and he is immeasurably grateful for this kindness, for her patient affection—but he will never tell her that! Instead, he will work in the bakery from morning until night without complaint, bearing the physical labor, the financial worries, all of the worries.

Morning coffee, black. Two fried eggs and a brötchen for breakfast. Lunch at 10:00 a.m., when possible. Meat, whatever is left over from last night's dinner. Maybe a piece of fruit. And bread, of course. The bread he could make in his sleep, and maybe sometimes he does. Occasionally he looks up from his work and it's hours later than he thought it was, and he has been baking—sifting, measuring, sprinkling, salting, kneading—as if in a dream.

Of course he hasn't been sleep-baking, but time does disappear for him, and he is, in that way, an artist, a man whose work is, by coincidence, his calling. He is fortunate, has always been fortunate, except for the great moment in his life when he was profoundly unfortunate, and maybe that's how luck works: perhaps there are some men who balance the ledger sheet every day, who work at jobs they neither like nor dislike, who come home to families they are tolerably fond of; who wake, in the morning, neutral about the day's prospects and fall into bed, hours later, depleted. And then there are men like Julius, who are given great full buckets of good luck in their lives: married to a woman of tender patience, father to a daughter who shines like the sun, owner of a prosperous business; he takes so much satisfaction in the emotional and tactile pleasures of his life and his work that sometimes he has to stand still just for a moment in the middle of the day, in the midst of the chaos, and pause for what would be, if he were a different kind of man, a prayer.

Deep down Julius harbors the secret and unreasonable hope that his quantity of bad luck has already been meted out to him, that Paul's death, when they were very young, was his portion.

When, on the first day of April, 1933—a chilly, sunny Saturday, typically the sort of day on which the bakery does a brisk business—the men stand outside the front window, he almost pities them. Feldenheim is a small city, and these three young men, decked out in their paramilitary finest as if for a costume party—high black boots and those foppish little brimmed hats—might very well be sons of his neighbors, or classmates of Annelise (they are just the right age), or children of his loyal customers, boys he has *fed,* with warm bread that he made with his own hands.

And now here they stand, shivering, their wisps of breath visible in the crisp spring air, acting like fools, like bullies, warning people to stay away, singing, chanting, trying to intimidate his regular customers. Succeeding, sometimes. But Julius doesn't have it in him to hate these boys. He just doesn't. In fact, he has half a mind to step outside and offer them warm brötchen, a vanillekipferl or two, a bit of nurturing. They want to belong to something, and so they belong to this, but maybe his kindness could suggest another option.

Their low, urgent chanting carries in from the street, music without melody. *Germans! Defend yourselves! Do not buy from Jews!* His head bent over a baking sheet, he feels the humiliation suddenly crash into him. He's not going to alter their hateful opinions by offering them warm pastries; he's not going to change the world with a cookie. The bell above the door rings to announce an entrance, and, for the first time, his heart jolts with fear at the sound of it, and he braces himself.

But it's a customer, a man he doesn't recognize who has pushed past the boys outside and stepped into the warmth of his bakery. He is middle-aged and polite, impersonal, takes off his hat, peers for a minute at the baked goods, just going about his morning errands. Julius feels so grateful to this stranger that his eyes fill and he has to turn away for a moment to collect himself. He adds a few extra buchteln to the order. The man nods at Julius, turns, and leaves.

The day brings few customers. At the end of it, after these boys have gone home (to their mothers? to dinner?), so much is left over, brötchen and brezeln and mohnkuchen, an entire käsekuchen Berta Baumann ordered but did not pick up. There is so much goodness—beauty—in these breads and pastries; Julius still thinks that. They are sustenance and pleasure, his gift. He gathers them, wraps the cake, packs everything into a paper bag to give to the beggars he'll pass on his way home.

Alone (he heard the rumors and told everyone else to stay home), he closes the shop in the dim light, under a pall of unease. He walks home for dinner, head down, hurrying as if through a foreign city.

Klara greets him in the doorway. Her hands shake as she takes his coat. There were beatings in the streets. They stayed inside all day, she tells him.

That night Julius dreams about his brother. When Paul appears to him, facedown in the creek, a tiny boy in shallow water, Julius wakes up, as he always does, his heart pounding, his breathing shallow (almost as if he is the drowning one). Paul's death was a shattering. Julius was too young to make sense of it, and grief, even after all this time, is still a lonely surprise. He wakes and knows without touching it that his face is wet.

Klara, who has been his witness for twenty-five years, draws her husband closer in half-sleep.

I was terribly upset in Frankfurt when we said good-bye.

A thirty-one-year-old man will come with some history, and Walter's is named Johanna.

Johanna is another in the endless parade of tall, finely featured women who stride through Annelise's life, a marching band of beauties—Katarina; her best friend, Sofie; and now this one, Johanna, stunning and aloof. Next to them, Annelise feels like a shrub.

She knows Walter and Johanna Goldmann the way she knows everyone else—they're regular customers at the bakery. They come in several days a week at 4:00 on the dot for *Kaffee und Kuchen*. Walter has the formal good manners of someone who has never had cause to doubt his worth.

On their first day in the neighborhood, he introduces himself and Johanna, solemnly and with unexpected sweetness. "We're new to this area, and I think we'll be coming here often," he says, and he makes a gesture toward the glass case, to the selection of cakes and pastries; and, possibly, although neither of them knows it, that sweep of his arm extends up, above the counter, all the way to her.

Johanna stands next to him, gazing at him, silent, her little *Mona Lisa* smile a full suit of armor.

You can serve some customers every day and never notice them; others make their indelible mark immediately, for no clear reason, except that maybe you are, by some strange magic, paying very close attention.

Walter orders—schwarzwälder kirschtorte for him, bienenstich for her—and he pulls out a chair at one of the little round tables in the corner, makes sure his wife is seated, that everything she needs is right in front of her, before he sits down. They stay for just over an hour, taking their sweet time at the table. It's a Tuesday, not very busy. Annelise watches them discreetly. They lean into each other as if their conversation is a jewel they're forming together, as if they're alchemists.

Some days, Johanna hurries in in the morning by herself, full of purpose, and buys the bread she needs for the day. Annelise wraps her package and thinks with a little pang that this means that she won't be seeing Walter later, although, really, why should she care? Johanna is friendly enough when she's with her husband, but alone, she looks past Annelise, searching for more interesting people who might be behind her. (But of course only Annelise's parents are behind her, bustling about in the kitchen, preparing cake batter and kneading bread dough and arguing companionably about how much salt to use, or the freshness of the milk. Their arguments are melodies; fifty years later, Annelise will still be able to hear them.) Sometimes Johanna taps her round red fingernails on the glass counter if Annelise is taking too long to wrap her brötchen or make change. She is one of those women whose husbands bring out the best in them; their trick is that everyone knows that except the husbands.

*

Walter was in the habit (slightly disconcerting, he was aware) of staring at Johanna while she slept. He knew if she woke up and found him lying there, as still and unblinking as a reptile, studying her beautiful face, she'd be annoyed, possibly even angry, but he couldn't help it. She was glorious, ethereal, a *Weisse Frau*. Her face invited scrutiny—no, required it! She was a goddess, and he, Walter Goldmann, was nothing but mortal. He was affable, certainly, but he considered himself relentlessly average: on the short side, myopic, prone to worry. He had always felt that his ears were too big. He was a shoe salesman with a primary school education, for goodness' sake. Johanna had landed in his lumpen life, shimmering and bright, and he could not believe his good luck. He memorized her face so that, if she ever left him (he worried; he was a *worrier*), at least her image would remain.

They met in his shoe store. He told people he was a shoe salesman, and it was true, but it was also true that he owned the store. She came in one morning, early, full of purpose, strode over to Erich, the timid young clerk who had been working there for only three weeks. "Show me a selection of your most beautiful shoes," she said, tapping on the counter. "Money is no object."

Erich hiccupped and hurried back to the stockroom for Walter, who could charm the most demanding ladies.

She sat down on a high red chair and pretended it was a throne, a trick that had been working for her since childhood. In the end, after trying on shoes for over an hour, after Walter worked up a sweat trying to please her (a harbinger of things to come; he thrilled to it, even then), Johanna chose a pair of black and purple brocade T-straps with interwoven stripes and a Cuban heel, pricey and stylish and impractical. Walter wrapped the shoes as Johanna removed bills from her beaded purse, one by one: her father's money, pilfered from his bureau. He would not miss it.

She walked around the small store one more time, slowly, lightly touching a few of the shoes on display, glancing back at Walter, who was watching her with an expectant look on his face. Their hour together had been intimate. There was no other word for a man's strong hand taking the shape of a woman's foot. Her initial embarrassment took her by surprise; twenty minutes later, she had conquered it.

She had stormed out of her house that morning, incensed. Her father had called her *frivolous,* her mother had demanded that she start taking her life seriously. They had clear ideas about her future, the cache of well-brought-up men from which she would be allowed to choose—from which, they insisted, it was time for her to choose. She didn't care for any of them, the arrogant Heinrichs and smug Horsts. She was capable of making her own decisions.

She met the shoe salesman's eye: a tradesman, a business owner. Walter Goldmann. Goldmann! Ha! She appraised his face in her frank way. How better to prove to her family that she would not be bullied than by bringing home a man like this? She laughed out loud. Walter heard bells ringing.

He had been seeing a lovely young woman named Rosa Grünbaum. They were strolling calmly, chastely toward marriage. He broke it off hours after meeting Johanna. She was a comet. He was blinded by her light.

But she was not just these things, not only fire and spite. She was generous, and thoughtful, and determined. She craved her family's approval and tiptoed right up to the limits of it, then leapt.

They were married in a civil ceremony. Walter had no family, and Johanna's didn't come. He didn't understand until too late that he was a specific ingredient in her messy concoction. By the time it made sense to him, he was so deeply in love with Johanna that he would have done anything for her, anything to get her family's consent. Nothing he offered made a difference to them, of course.

He stared at her as she slept. She breathed like a kitten, little mewls and purrs. Her fine, light hair was a tangle on her pillow. She pinned it up at night, but it invariably slipped out of its clips; she raised her hand to her head every morning and cursed the mess of it. He adjusted his body, moved as close to her as he could without waking her.

It was such a privilege to lie with someone, to hold a person's changing form in the drift and sweetness of sleep.

The early morning light was intensifying. Johanna snored softly and stirred. Her eyes blinked open, and Walter watched as she became herself.

"Why are you looking at me?" Her morning voice was a croak. She laughed and put her palm over his face, pretended to push him away. He kissed the soft middle of her hand, wrapped his arms around his wife, and existed, just briefly, without thoughts in this rare and perfect moment.

Two years in, Johanna realized she couldn't live without her family's acceptance, her father's approval. That was the end of them. They had not yet had children. It was, in that way only, a clean break.

They had been man and wife. He knew her secrets and her details: that she was bitterly jealous of her little sister, Christine, that she hated pickles, that she loved jazz. He had run his thumb gently over the mole on her right shoulder. He knew the burnt-caramel smell of her.

After she left him, he didn't want to know anything else. In Germany, for those few years he still lived there, and then after, he avoided asking questions of people who might have had a connection to Johanna or any information about her life: whom she'd married (she had surely remarried), whether she had children, how she lived out those particular years. Even Oskar, his closest friend in Feldenheim, who had known them as a couple, he forbade from mentioning her. In his adopted American city of German immigrants, where everybody knew someone from home, he deliberately avoided asking. He did this so that, now and then, he would be able to think of her with some fondness.

Years later, admiring his dark-haired daughter, the light of his life, in the city he wouldn't have been able to find on a map back when he lived in Germany, he understood that even pain could bring joy. It wasn't a trade-off, and it didn't give him comfort; it was just something true.

Please write and answer all of my questions, and don't be lax about writing, because this is all that we have left of you.

They stop coming to the bakery after about six months. It occurs to Annelise as she is sweeping up a flour spill that she hasn't seen the couple in a while, and a quick electrical current buzzes through her; she realizes that she misses Walter's face, his gentle manners, and equally that she does not miss Johanna's haughty efficiency. And then she can't recall the last time she's seen them. Has it been weeks? Has it been months?

A few days later, as if drawn by her thoughts, the bells above the door jingle, and Walter slouches in. She glances up and doesn't recognize him at first—he looks so much thinner, older. There are dark smudges under his brown eyes.

"How may I help you?" Annelise asks, and then, "Oh! Hello!" and then, with a tiny, unintentional grimace, "And where is your lovely wife today?"

There is no one else in the bakery. It's almost closing time. The dusk still makes Annelise melancholy. Although she is well over Max, has finished mourning him for good, in fact barely even thinks about him, the truth is that it's been three years and there has been no one since him, and so, for her, the lasting imprint of love is sadness.

Walter looks down, pretends to examine the sparse contents of the bakery case. It's an unseasonably warm day in early May, and he takes a white handkerchief from his pocket and wipes a little trickle of perspiration from his forehead.

"Ah . . . Johanna is gone," he says after a pause, and with such sorrow that Annelise, without thinking, reaches across the counter and touches his hand.

"I'm so sorry," she murmurs. "She was so young. How . . . how did she . . . ?"

Walter laughs. Annelise pulls away and plants her hands furiously on her hips, does her best to cool her boiling humiliation. Who is this man, laughing at his wife's demise? Her sympathies shift, suddenly and completely, to poor, dead Johanna, brought irrevocably low by marriage to this monster.

"No, no, my wife is not dead," he says, color rising in his cheeks now. "We're . . . Johanna and I are, we're divorced." He lifts one shoulder, a little punctuation mark.

Annelise holds his gaze. There is, of course, a certain appeal to a broken man. "Well, I'm still sorry," she says, "although I suppose not as sorry as I was when I thought she was dead."

Walter stares at her for another second, eyebrows raised, and then he laughs again, and, to Annelise's surprise, he keeps laughing until he has to wipe away the tears from his eyes.

Annelise stands with her elbows bent, hands still on her hips, and observes Walter—the crinkly lines around his eyes, his face entirely open to happiness.

The irregular beat of her heart is the first uncertain thump of love.

Today I had a very difficult day. I was so homesick for all of you.

Please write in your next letter whether I should sell my stone pots. I may have somebody who wants to buy them. For the time being I won't buy anything, for, as you wrote, it could still take about a year or so until we can leave here, and who knows what can happen.

Thank you for the beautiful picture of Ruthie. She looks like such a bright little girl. She looks so much older and has a much different expression on her face. Why does she have to be so far away from us?

Dear Lise, nobody can change anything. You looked that way when you were that age, my dear child.

Later, he'll marvel at their small slice of good luck: that they fell in love before the fear sank down into their bones. It was a small thing, to get to know each other as they were. It was a gift.

Certain events diminish you, alter your elemental structure. Later, he will not trust police officers; she won't abide Fourth of July parades. She'll shrink from conflict; he'll refuse to sleep under a window. He'll suffer panic attacks. She'll hate the language she feels most comfortable speaking. That's who they'll become.

But when they fell in love, they were just who they were.

"He's ten years older than I am," Annelise warns her parents.

Her father slides his knife into a baked potato with gusto. "None of the impulsiveness of a younger man," he says. Klara looks fondly at Julius and nods.

"He's been married before," Annelise says. Her mother passes the butter dish to her father and dabs her mouth with a napkin. It's as if they can't hear her. "He is *divorced!*"

"He must have been very young," Klara says. She pours water from a crystal pitcher into her husband's glass, then her own.

"Well, she wasn't Jewish!" Annelise says, saving her best argument for last. "His wife was not Jewish!"

"Not uncommon these days," her father says, now carving his roast chicken into small pieces.

"Remedied, perhaps," her mother adds, with an infuriating wink.

What is she trying to do? She's fond of Walter. She's enamored of him! He's good and lovely, handsome and so attentive. He looks at her when she talks. He remembers her favorite song ("I Kiss Your Hand, Madame," from the movie) and sings little snippets to her in her ear. He offers his arm to her as they walk down the street and then smoothly maneuvers her body so that he's the one walking on the outside, closer to traffic. He is solicitous and sweet. He reminds her of Julius.

"Invite him to dinner," her father says. They acknowledge him when he comes to the bakery, of course. But they're people who believe in rules.

Her mother nods. "Next week," she demands.

A few nights later, they're walking home from a film. The evening is misty and damp. Their footsteps sound like the last echoing applause in an empty theater.

"My mother and father," Annelise says, removing her hand from Walter's in order to smooth her hair, renegade in the humidity. "Klara and Julius." She had the idea that saying their first names would make her seem mature, and she immediately feels idiotic. "They have insisted that . . . no, I mean, have *asked* that . . . and of course I would also like it, if you . . ." Her confidence fizzles in a lightning zap. She glances around, as if she might find it lying on the cobbled sidewalk. "We would like it if you would join us . . ."

"Of course," Walter says. "I'd be delighted." *Well, finally,* he thinks.

On his way to Lise's apartment to meet her parents, Walter pauses at a poster tacked to a lamppost. THE JEWS ARE OUR MISFORTUNE! it reads, and his first reaction (which he will also ponder later, frequently) is an audible chuckle. He has a keen eye for absurdity, which doesn't always work in his favor. *Whose,* he wonders, and *how?* He's a shoe salesman. He sells *shoes.* People compliment his high-quality selection and frequent his thriving business. They appreciate his competitive prices! He is a valuable member of the community, a sincere if irregular synagogue attendee, a conscientious shopkeeper who sweeps snow not only from the front steps of his own store, but also from those of the businesses on either side. He does the weekly shopping for two of his elderly neighbors. He sets out a bowl of milk for the stray kitten that likes to climb up to his kitchen windowsill. And he doesn't even particularly like cats!

Walter straightens his back and moves past the lamppost, tucking the two bouquets of flowers he's carrying closer to his chest—a spray of lavender tulips for Mrs. Adler and a dozen red roses for Annelise. Tulips, he feels, are respectful, subdued, and long-lasting, just the impression he is hoping to make. Red roses—he knows what they mean. He's crazy about Annelise, and even if she hasn't quite arrived at the same conclusion, he knows that she will. He is nobody's misfortune.

It's dusk. The gas lamps are flickering on. He passes a few workers heading home, a young couple, arm in arm. The man nods at him, and Walter touches the brim of his hat in reply. He walks quickly now past shops and buildings so familiar they're etched into his brain in their particular order—Woolworth's, grocer, dry goods, coffee shop, doctor's office—the collage of home he will return to in his dreams. The night is close, and a little perspiration gathers on his forehead. He takes out his handkerchief and wipes it away. By the time he arrives at the Adlers' apartment building, he is just slightly out of breath and has put that poster out of his head almost completely.

She feels like a little girl, sitting here in her parents' living room, her own home, surrounded by the detritus of her intimate life. The dolls on the shelf in her bedroom. Wolfgang, the one-eyed stuffed bear lying languid and winking on her bed. The bathroom down the hall, the toilet! How has she allowed herself to invite Walter into such mortifying proximity? Even this living room. A framed photograph of her as a small child. Her cello stand. The lamp she broke when she was five (repaired, the crack down the middle of the stand barely visible). The wingback chair she likes to curl up and read in. Walter sits across from her, taking in the room for the first time, and suddenly to Annelise her home feels like an excavation site of her childhood. She is not ready for this.

What are they talking about? She's drifted. Her father and Walter are drinking brandy, their gestures, she notices, mirroring each other's.

"We're treated with less respect," her father is saying.

"Some suspicion," Walter agrees. He debates telling them about the poster. He's seen a few others like it around town. He suspects they all have. Murmurs, whispers. A cloud hanging over them, but tempered with faith in the prevailing sanity of their friends and fellow citizens.

"I was standing in line at the butcher shop," her mother offers, sitting down, finally. "And Mr. Günther only waited on me after he'd served the very last person in line, a woman who'd arrived fifteen minutes after I had. The very last person. 'Next customer, please. Next customer, please.'" She waves her hand, shooing an imaginary person aside. "Imagine!" she says.

Annelise has nothing to add to the conversation. She absently fingers her brooch and looks over at Walter, who is alternating his intent gaze between her parents.

She shifts in her chair and feels a little trickle of blood moving through her. In school, Emmi and Sofie would whisper their dramatic complaints every month: the hassle, the extra washing, the inconvenience of it. They were always so *exasperated* by it. But Lise finds it fascinating. How remarkable to be able to chart your own internal course, to receive a regular reminder from your body: you are here, you are ready.

Walter and her parents are still talking, although they seem to have changed subjects, thankfully. A mutual friend in Belgium? The weather? A mutual friend enjoying the weather in Belgium? She crosses her legs and closes her eyes for a second and sees a negative image of the living room in front of her: fireplace, bookcase, table lamps glowing, mirror, her parents, Walter.

She feels herself growing more distracted, fighting the distinct feeling that she's done this before, that her life is both hers and not hers, slight jolts surrounded by cotton wool.

He really is so good and lovely. And handsome. Dark hair, dark eyes, his dark-gray suit. He takes her to dinner every week, sometimes to a concert or a film. He asks her opinion on everything and does not talk too much about shoes. During those evenings she wonders if he will surprise her. He's been to France, twice. He talks about Berlin, as Max had, but as a place to visit. She likes his gathering laughter, his instinct to laugh.

She runs her toe along the edge of the rug beneath her chair and notices that the living room has fallen silent.

"What do you think, Annelise?" her mother asks, and Annelise blushes.

"I'm sorry! I wasn't paying attention," she says, and then after a moment she laughs, because it doesn't matter; she knows she is loved by everyone in the room.

"Our dreamer," her father says.

Walter meets her eyes. "I will have to work on my conversational skills," he says, and Annelise thinks she can feel the heat from him, the love he feels for her, and the wanting.

"No," her mother says, her hand on Walter's arm, squeezing. "Your conversational skills are delightful!" She presses her lips together and glares at Annelise. "Aren't they, Lise?" Her father raises his glass to Walter and drinks.

It's almost comical, the way they're releasing her to him. They make it seem inevitable. But nothing is inevitable, not one single thing, not the kind of jam you spread on your toasted bread in the morning nor the way you tuck your hair behind your ear at the exact second he is looking at you, nor the moment two bodies come together to conceive a child, particular and astonishing.

Her mother's hand still rests on Walter's arm. Her father leans forward in his chair, offers their guest more brandy.

Annelise feels an ancient pull toward safety. A bottle clinks to a glass. In the room there is quiet assent, a low murmuring.

I have sorted your things, Lise. I will send them.

The first time she's pregnant, Annelise feels like a member of a secret club. Even before the growing baby inside her is visible to anyone but her and Walter, she walks around her neighborhood, noticing the other members of the Secret Society of the Life-Givers (or, possibly, depending on the day, the Sisterhood of the Swollen Ankles): women who furtively touch a palm to their bellies or place a steadying hand on their aching backs; women so large and heavy they look like they might give birth right there on the sidewalk; women with barely rounded stomachs who pause, stop to shake a stone out of a shoe or pretend to study a street sign—the ones who, like her, need to rest for a moment, sit on a bench and catch their breath.

And she notices, too, all the children—how did they just appear like that, out of nowhere?—all of the beautiful children and the strange, plump, wobbling toddlers; the drooling, gummy babies gnawing on damp remnants of bread rolls; the fat, laughing babies and the silently staring ones. And (although this really shouldn't shock her) they all have mothers—coiffed women with thin lips, tired eyes; harried women with quick reflexes, hands on their children's heads, arms, shoulders, wrists (*stay here! Stay right here!*); tranquil women whose soft bodies are like furniture for their babies, like pillowy sofas.

They are everywhere, these children and their mothers, and Annelise never saw any of them before. But now she does. Now she sees them. And the patient mothers will hold their arms open to her. She will fall into this great chasm gently, and be received.

Her own mother has been in a tizzy of excitement since they told her the news, stopping by every day to add to the list of things the baby will need. But they're six months away from needing anything for this baby, and Annelise has to bite her lip to stop herself from telling her to please calm down.

(Her own mother: of course they've worked side by side at the bakery, and Klara has cooked for her and wrapped her sandwiches in kitchen paper and washed her clothes and nagged her to sweep the floor and kissed her forehead and run a hand down her unruly hair with an exasperated *tsk,* but it has never occurred to Annelise that this is motherhood. If she does consider Klara, it's with a suffusion of ineffable feeling rather than careful analysis, and in that rush of feeling is the sense that she *is* her mother—that when she looks in the mirror and sees her own face, she sees Klara's face, too, although not literally, because they don't look alike. Their connection is a deep and wordless blend of boiled potatoes and unsolicited advice, a lullaby about a dog, a sick stomach gently rubbed in the middle of the night, an argument about a hat: vexation and resentment and warmth and need, a viscous flow of liquid, imperfect love.)

The weeks go by slowly. Four months along, she feels the first flutters, so easily mistaken for something else, but unmistakably what they are. *Hello,* she thinks. It's thrilling and almost preposterous.

Her energy drains, but her vision sharpens. She sees the deadly risks and danger she'd been impervious to before: cars and bicycles whizzing past her on busy streets, trees with heavy, low-hanging branches, men who narrow their eyes and look too long. The bench she liked to sit on, outside the fruit market, that she is no longer permitted to sit on.

(The municipal parks she is no longer allowed to enjoy. The restaurants at which she may no longer dine. The swimming pools where, should she desire a cool dip, she may not swim. She exists—they all do—in this liminal state of bitter confusion, in the warped moment of watching a water glass slip out of a hand, staring at the winking shards that had been, seconds ago, solid, the memory of the drinking glass more real, more true, than its fragments.)

She sleeps late one Tuesday morning—a delicious luxury she allows herself now that she is married and no longer works at the bakery, one of the few she'll indulge in for the rest of her life. She wakes slowly, untangles herself from a dream, yawns, stretches. She opens her bedroom curtains and sees a long-limbed child wearing only underwear playing in the courtyard. He looks up, and for a second, their eyes meet, then he bends and gathers a clump of dirt in his fist, brings it up to his face. He shoves some of the dirt into his mouth, licks his lips, smiles at her. A little ball of fear forms in her chest. She imagines a wolf mama slipping through the fence, hot breath of raw meat, skulking into the courtyard to collect her child.

A moment later, a human mother in a flowered skirt rushes over to him and scoops him up, and Annelise hears the boy's feral scream.

Later that day she meets her old school friend Sofie, half-way between their two apartment buildings, on a quiet, shady street. The wolf-boy is still on Annelise's mind. She had scanned the courtyard as she left her building, peered up at the apartment windows, recalling his high-pitched howl. The fear she felt when she first saw him has dissipated but isn't gone, has only transformed from a solid mass into smoky wisps of unease.

Sofie is six months pregnant with her second child, cheerfully overwhelmed and lately bursting with advice for her friend about what kinds of sun bonnets are best, how to use gripe water for colic, when to rock a baby to sleep and when to let him cry.

Annelise waves from a half-block away. Sofie touches her finger to her lips as they near each other. Her two-year-old daughter, Inge, is asleep in her wicker push stroller, dark eyelashes like delicate petals against her pale cheeks, her head lolling to the side. Annelise stands on her tiptoes to kiss her tall friend on the cheek, then bends to press her lips gently to Inge's sweaty little forehead. They've chosen this quiet street because they can ramble at their own slow pace, and also because there are fewer reminders of the places Annelise can no longer go.

Their friendship is not a meeting of minds. Annelise is fully aware of this. It has never been the kind of rare, startling connection that makes a person feel lucky and seen—the kind of connection she once had with Max, but she long ago became adept at sweeping thoughts like that from her mind. It's not even the sort of witty, complementary bond she has with Emmi. Annelise and Sofie's friendship is easy and comforting, a stew cooked for a long time over a low flame. They are gentle and affectionate with each other, their friendship kept alive by the shared pleasure of predictable milestones. Sofie, who got married at eighteen, just after she graduated from the Gymnasium, coached Annelise through her wedding preparations, and, a few days before the ceremony, sat her down and gravely explained the mechanics of sex as if she were carefully informing her friend that someone had died.

"It will be . . . unpleasant at first," Sofie said, shaking her pretty blond head slowly and then more vigorously, her lips pursed. "Not what you'd expect." She widened her green eyes theatrically. "But then just when you think you're doomed, just when you think it's the price you have to pay for being married to the man you love . . ." She paused, put her hand over her mouth, giggled. "It becomes quite a bit more enjoyable!"

Annelise just nodded, trying to look shocked, letting Sofie play the worldly sophisticate, letting her think that she, Annelise, was as innocent as a lamb. The truth was that Walter was ten years older than Annelise, and divorced, and they had been together for more than a year before they got engaged. Sofie's life lesson was neither groundbreaking information nor, thankfully, particularly accurate to her experience.

"Oh, goodness," she whispered as Sofie patted her arm. "Oh, my!" She thought about trying to make herself cry, but decided that would be taking things a step too far. "I'm speechless," Annelise said, and coughed to cover a little snort of laughter.

But there was only so much conversation to be squeezed from shared moments and unnecessary life lessons, and the two friends had, over the past year, been running out of things to talk about. Annelise was starting to dread their time together, Sofie's long, mundane discussions about infant feeding schedules and diaper changing punctuated by awkward silences, but just as she had started practicing excuses to avoid seeing Sofie, her pregnancy infused new energy into their relationship.

"I'm so hungry!" Annelise announces, falling into rhythm next to Sofie. "I'm just starving all the time now! I wish I'd brought an apple or something. Do you have one?" Sofie shakes her head. "I could eat Inge's stroller," she says, laughing. "I could eat Inge! Those pudgy little feet of hers, those cheeks!"

Inge's overwhelming perfection has become a common refrain: *Have you noticed how cute her toes are? Look at how her hair curls on the ends, like angel floss.* Inge is, indeed, lovely, although perhaps not as lovely as all that, but it's not hard for Annelise to play along, to find common ground in this child; it brings the two friends closer. Which is why it's so strange that Sofie is not participating now, not adding to the conversation the way she normally does—*I know, and how about those sweet hands, like little knödel!*

Annelise turns to Sofie. "Not feeling hungry today, love?"

Sofie shakes her head slightly. Inge makes a small sound, and

Sofie gasps, fusses with the little girl's ruffled collar, smooths her hair, whispers, *Shhhh*.

"Annelise," she says after a minute. Her voice is high, clenched. "I have to tell you something." Sofie touches her own hair nervously, readjusts a pin. "I have to tell you . . ." She runs a finger over first her left eyebrow, then her right, as if she is primping in front of a mirror. "Lise, I . . . I'm sorry . . . I really can't be your friend anymore."

Annelise stops breathing for one imploded second. She is not stupid, not blind.

By the time she can inhale again, Sofie is ten steps ahead of her.

"Sofie," Annelise calls, keeping her voice light, reaching for just the right tone. "Sofie, honestly! Of course you can be my friend. You *are* my friend. What are you talking about?"

Sofie stops and turns to Annelise. She has the excellent posture of someone who has been lucky all her life. From an apartment somewhere above them, a baby—*another one*—cries. A curtain is drawn in a window beside them. It's midday, warm. They are alone, together, in the middle of the shady sidewalk.

Her beautiful friend: blond hair in finger waves, violet maternity dress draped over her belly, tears streaming down her face. "It's not . . . it's not you." She's sobbing now, choking the words out. "Martin says we can't. He says it's bad for the family, bad for Inge, and this new baby, our growing family." Sofie is swiping tears from her face. Her nose is running, her makeup smearing darkly under her eyes. She looks pathetic, pitiful; Annelise reaches out, and Sofie does not move Annelise's hand from her arm; she barrels right past this gesture of impossible sympathy. "You . . . I mean. Because you're . . . well, you're. You're not a good influence." She rummages for a handkerchief in her handbag, blows her nose. "Martin says it's not your fault. He says it's not you, Lise— you're different, he knows that. He likes you! But it's in your blood. You can't deny it." Sofie is wracked with sobs now, destroyed.

Annelise has celebrated every Christmas since she was seven years old with Sofie's family. She has brought over lebkuchen and marzipan stollen that Klara lovingly baked for them. She has sat in the good parlor with Sofie's parents and her brother Kurt and eaten Christmas turkey with them, and she has listened, for almost two decades, to her friend talk—incessantly, as a matter of fact—about herself. She stood next to Sofie at her wedding, and she has held Inge in her arms more times than she can count and she has accepted kisses on the cheek from Sofie's husband, Martin, and has ignored—like a true friend!—the way, at the end of an evening, those wet wormy lips of his like to migrate toward her mouth.

"You're not a good influence," Sofie says again, nodding with the inevitable truth of it, this dreadful admission, her handkerchief balled up in her fist, shoulders hunched over the handles of the push stroller.

"But Inge is only two!" Annelise says, as if that's the point. Sofie's sobs are little hiccups now, birdlike peeps. She won't look at Annelise, just stands there, clutching the handles of the stroller.

Annelise is wilting in the heat of the day, the hunger she arrived with replaced suddenly with overwhelming thirst. *Poor Sofie,* she thinks. *Poor, poor Sofie.* She walks over to Sofie and puts her arms around her friend, her friend a moment ago but no longer, her once and former friend. Sofie smells like lemon eau de toilette and salty sweat, a disagreeable mix; Annelise sees, up close, a greasy sheen of perspiration on her forehead, her upper lip.

Annelise is transforming, she thinks, right here, into something else, something sturdy and resigned. She thought marriage made her an adult, she thought pregnancy made her a woman, but no, it's this moment, right now, in the middle of the sidewalk, hot and thirsty and embracing her stupid friend.

"It's all right," she murmurs, less forgiveness than temporary indifference. Sophie's hard, round belly bumps up against her own soft flesh. She feels no grief, no loss, just this awkward abutting. "It's all right," she says again, and Sofie nods—it will always be all right for Sofie!—her chin sharp against Annelise's head. Annelise moves around to the front of the stroller and bends toward the flushed, sleeping toddler. Inge's green eyes and her rosebud lips are her mother's; her squashed nose, high, translucent forehead, and thin, wispy hair unmistakably her father's. If she sees this little girl again, it will be only in passing, never again up close. "Bye, darling," Annelise whispers to her. And then, from somewhere deep and savage, Annelise reaches over and pinches the sleeping child on the thigh, hard. Hard, hard, hard.

Inge wakes up screaming and, through her hot, dazzled tears and against the inexplicable throbbing of her thigh, the confused child sees the narrow back of her mother's best friend walking swiftly down the sidewalk, away.

A week later, someone hurls a brick through Walter and Annelise's dining room window. It crashes through the glass, arcs through the air, gouges a deep chunk out of the corner of their polished mahogany table, and comes to rest amid glass shards and wood splinters on the floor.

Three days after that, Annelise wakes up in an explosion of pain and blood, howling. Her pregnancy is over, her baby is gone.

Of all the ways her heart will break, the most negligible one will be that Sofie will never know.

Nothing but bad luck.

Lise, I think that you look a little sad in the picture.

There's nothing we can do about it. The worries just don't

go away.

———

This is a love story.

Clare mostly dated Jewish men, despite her constitutional aversion to religion. But the city was small, and it was challenging to avoid boys she'd gone to kindergarten with.

There was one she liked, a social worker at the veterans hospital who had just moved to town. They went to a movie, and afterward, when the lights came up, he pretended to read her palm. He traced a line across her hand. "You find me irresistible," he said, then looked up at her, grinning.

Later that night they were facing each other on her bed. She touched the side of his neck. His hand was in her hair. He kissed her. She felt a little tug against the tangle of her curls, then a harder pull. Was his hand *stuck?* He stopped, carefully extricated his fingers from her hair. "You remind me of another," he murmured in her ear, and they resumed kissing.

She stopped again, pushed him away. "Wait, did you just say I remind you of your mother?"

He looked at her. Laughed, embarrassed.

"Your *mother?*"

"I'm sorry. It's not a bad thing?" He shrugged. Jake. He was nice, though. He would end up marrying one of his coworkers, a woman named Tracee, from Oshkosh. He would live a happy life, minus bad knees and elevated cholesterol and chronic insomnia and premature baldness and a certain ineffable restlessness. He would lie awake most nights, worrying about the veterans and his two sons and his receding gums and the crisis at the border while Tracee (*who was she? how was this possible?*) slept peacefully beside him.

Clare scooted to the edge of her bed. "Oh, no, I have to, um . . ." His *mother.* She was exposed, humiliated, a hippo in a tutu. She got up, tucked in her shirt, ran her hands down the cute pink skirt she'd picked out for this date.

She swore off all men after that, for a while.

There was another one, a lanky graduate student in the biology department (she was in literature, two floors up). They had lunch together once in a while. They talked about their families. They had several mutual friends, as all the Jews in Milwaukee did. He didn't seem interested in her, but she thought maybe he just didn't realize he was. It was such a familiar script. Once, as he was finishing his turkey sandwich, he said, "C, I have a question for you." He nervously tore off a bit of crust, and her heart thwonked like a broken washing machine. "Do you think you could set me up with your friend Nina?"

There was the graphic designer who wouldn't stop talking about superheroes. The vegan who scowled when Clare ordered a cheese omelet. The med student who talked about himself for ninety minutes straight. It went on like that.

Her mother never said a word, but Clare thought she could see the clock inside her brain, anxiously ticking away—weeks, months, years. She was twenty-three, twenty-six, now twenty-eight. She lived in a small apartment in the trendiest part of this untrendy city, studied, worked an administrative job, had dinner with her parents once a week. Year after year she accompanied them to High Holiday services, where her mother showed her off, *You remember my daughter,* beaming with pride, although Clare felt that she didn't really deserve it, since she was so single and so vague about her career aspirations: a human cloud, really, just floating around.

She could have lived anywhere after college, but, like her compulsion to date Jewish men and her belief that horizontal stripes were unflattering, she'd grown up with the implicit sense that it was best not to venture too far. So while her friends flung themselves across the world, she came back to Milwaukee and settled in. Maybe her mother was proud of *that.*

It wasn't like looking in a mirror. Ruth had dark hair and fair skin. She looked like the hero's undoing in a 1950s film noir. Clare took after her father's side, light-brown curly hair, deep-set hazel eyes, narrow face; in pictures, no matter how hard she tried, she wore the same weary smile she'd seen in every photograph ever smuggled out of a shtetl. But underneath their skin, she and her mother knew each other. They predicted each other's needs, moods, phone calls. It was a romance.

She had a standing dinner date at her parents' house every Sunday. She brought them a half-dozen bagels once, and her mother refused to accept them.

"Don't be silly," Ruth said, pressing the bag back into Clare's hands. "Dad and I can get our own bagels. You'll put these in your freezer and you'll have bagels for breakfast all week!" Which she did.

The day after the solipsistic med student she'd been dating

for four months broke up with her, Clare toyed with the idea of canceling on her parents. But she was hungry. She decided on the drive over that she would not tell her mother about the breakup.

At the door, Ruth pulled Clare in for a hug. She sniffed Clare's head and said, "What's wrong?" and simultaneously reached around her to beckon to Clare's father, who was out in the yard raking leaves.

"Nothing's wrong." Oh, she couldn't. She couldn't bear the dripping excess of her mother's concern. She could not, at the worst of it, tolerate the burden of her mother's love-soaked sympathy, the wrinkles of empathetic worry permanently etching themselves into Ruth's pale skin.

"All right," her mother said. Then, "Dinner! Mel, did you see that your daughter's here? Dinner!"

Her father waved cheerfully at them and continued raking. He was wearing a red T-shirt and yellow Bermuda shorts and black dress socks. He looked like the flag of a small European country.

(Many years later, that was the outfit her father would be wearing when he appeared to Clare in a dream. "Dad," she would say to him, "why the dress socks?" and her father would chuckle and say, "Wouldn't you like to know," and Clare would say, "Yes! I would! I would like to know!" and her father, still chuckling, fading in the dream light, would shrug and say, "So would I," and she would wake up laughing at what felt like the sum of their father-daughter relationship, a steadfast and bewildering affection.)

"Look at him out there," Ruth said, then clucked her tongue

and closed the door. Her mother loved an ally against Mel's free-floating weirdness.

But Clare was too distracted to indulge, gnawing over one of the last things Zach the med student had said to her: *I'm sorry, I'm just not feeling it.*

"Feeling what?" she'd asked.

"It. This. Us," he said.

"Are you having a stroke?" Clare asked. Meanly. Porcupine quills out. Zach shook his head at her, frowned a disappointed frown. Pulled on his clothes and left.

She debated telling her mother, but she was too sad, too sad about that feckless aspiring urologist, and she knew that if she told Ruth, the floodgates would open, and her mother would take her into her arms and hold her while she cried.

"You'll find someone else," her mother would say.

And Clare would be furious, and also not any less sad.

She watched Ruth rinse lettuce. The tap was on full force, unleashing a waterfall over one head of iceberg lettuce. "Mom!" she said. "You're wasting water." But her mother didn't hear her over the sound of the water.

(Ruth did hear her, but she chose to ignore. She rinsed until she felt the lettuce was sufficiently rinsed, then turned the tap off.) "Do you want to stay over tonight, sweetie? I made up your bed, just in case."

"I have a thing tomorrow. But I don't know. Maybe." Clare slept so well in her childhood room, and woke up on a weekend morning to French toast. She was still so willing to be mothered.

"I can get you up early. You know how your father keeps me

awake with his snoring, so I'm not sleeping much anyway. I don't mind. I'll get you up whenever you need me to."

Clare sat down at the table, in the blue vinyl-covered chair she'd been sitting in her whole life. Her mother used to prop her on a phone book when she was too small to see over the edge. "Okay. Sure. I'll stay."

They clung to each other, refugees from an ancient sorrow. Right here in the suburbs, under a cloudless October sky!

"I made chocolate pudding," Ruth said, which had been Clare's favorite since she was a child, and was it still? Neither of them knew.

How did all of her friends suddenly decide it was time to get married? Was twenty-eight the age when a psychic switch was flipped, like getting your twelve-year molars? If you were one of the lucky ones, did you step out of your apartment and no matter what season it was, suddenly it was autumn, and you were the star of your own romantic comedy, and there he was, painting a mural on the side of your building, or in the grocery store reaching for the ripe avocado you had your hand on? Or maybe you just looked at the person you happened to be dating and said, "I guess we might as well do this."

Clare had spent long afternoons with her grandparents when she was a little girl, whiling away hours in their warm apartment, making spritz cookies with Annelise or playing gin rummy at the kitchen table with Walter while Annelise made lunch.

There was a small courtyard outside their building with a sandbox and a swing set, and there was a playground just down the street. Happy shouts and yelps punctuated their quiet afternoons. But Clare's was never a voice among the cacophony, because her grandparents wouldn't let her leave. The air in the apartment seemed to change whenever she asked, to grow staticky and strange. Her grandparents would exchange glances, a few words in German, and then her grandmother would say to her, "Oh, sweetheart, help me bake a cake, instead," or, "But I think Opa wants to do a puzzle with you!" And so she stopped asking and resigned herself to the quiet pleasures of the indoors. She was their tiny, precious captive. She gave herself over to it, to their hovering, and their love. She floated, unthinking, in the warm, liquid safety of it.

She grew into a mopey teenager: difficult to rouse in the mornings, reluctant to leave the house. She found it impossible to participate in the things that seemed to delight other girls—football games, parties, group shopping trips to the mall. None of it made sense to her. She slept until noon on bright fall days and on perfect summer ones, emerging from her dark bedroom only to complain about whatever mundane noise it was that had awakened her—a leaf blower, her father's singing, a bird.

"But what do you have to be sad about?" Ruth asked her once—not unkindly but truly baffled. She had everything. They had given her everything. "Why are you so *glum?*" And sixteen-year-old Clare, mute with misery, spread her arms wide to take in everything in the room, everything in the world.

She wondered, much later, if during those stretched-out days with her grandparents she might have taken on some of their sadness; if what they gave her, along with their love, was a grain of something that embedded itself inside her, that she protected, in spite of herself, with her body's hot sludge, until it was her own gorgeous, secret sorrow, nacreous and pearled.

And now here she was, adult and adrift. She went on dates that made her weary, and then she turned them into funny stories that she shared with her friends.

She was an astronaut, a cave dweller. Loneliness accrued around her, in the spaces between the coffee mugs in her cupboard, in the millimeters between the spines of her books, on her windowsills and under her bed. She could almost see its ghoulish eyes, its creeping fingers. She panicked, sometimes, in her apartment. Her pounding heart scrabbled at its cage.

She went out for dinner with the guy who fixed her computer. All evening long, she couldn't remember his name. But he smiled sweetly as he explained motherboards to her and asked her about her life. Adam, Brian, Chad. "I might go back for my master's," she said. David, Ethan. Fred? "But I'm not sure I'm really passionate about anything." Gary?

He nodded at her sympathetically. "I get that." He paused, took a bite of whatever it was he had ordered; she hadn't been paying attention. There was sauce. Cheese. "Although to be honest, I guess I am pretty stoked about computers."

She took a gulpy sip of water and stared down at her plate of spaghetti, hoping it might tell her what to say next.

Henry? tapped his fingers on the table. "Do you have any hobbies?" he asked.

"Not really," she said. "I read a lot. That probably doesn't count. What about you?"

"I'm building a computer from scratch," he said.

She laughed, then realized that he was not joking, and then he laughed, too. And she wondered, *Should I settle for the computer guy, here in the Italian restaurant?* Isaac, Josh, Ken, Lawrence. *Should I try that?* She couldn't help the long sigh that escaped from her mouth.

In the season of weddings, Liddy's was the first. She and Clare had been best friends since fourth grade. They'd made a pact when they were ten that they would live together as grown-ups in a glass house on a lake, where they would raise kittens and eat only Froot Loops. Much was expected of her, as Liddy's maid of honor, and in the months leading up to the wedding, Clare watched nervously as her paltry savings trickled away.

But of course there was a thrill to it, swooshing down the aisle in a swirl of teal chiffon, standing in front of two hundred guests and giving the speech that made the bride cry. ("I always thought we'd end up in that glass house together, so I'm holding you to it. We'll just have to add an extra room for Jason's drum equipment." Applause.) That first wedding was magical, full of promise and romance. She danced all night with a groomsman named Luke.

The sixth wedding was her college roommate's, on a riverboat in the Mississippi, where, for the entire reception, Clare stood alone at the railing, staring at the horizon and trying not to throw up. She almost made it.

In between, and gradually, at weddings two, three, four, and five, she became an anthropologist. Sometimes she was a bridesmaid, sometimes a guest at the singles table closest to the kitchen. She was gimlet-eyed and always lonely.

At her office mate's wedding, number five, she watched the bride and groom smear cake onto each other's faces. It seemed a little mean, but then everyone laughed and clapped, and they kissed. A blob of frosting plopped onto the bride's dress. Her office mate had met the man of her dreams at karaoke night, six weeks earlier.

They weren't so different from funerals, the weddings. Maybe everyone knew that, but it was a revelation to Clare. She recalled the line of tiny German women at her grandmother's funeral, how they approached Ruth and Clare, clutching first her mother's hands, then hers, murmuring, *My dear, my child.* If you squinted, it was all so much the same, the rush of love, the sadness lurking. She would never forget the look on Ruth's face that day, the love of a whole life turned to anguish.

At the riverboat wedding, a tipsy middle-aged man asked her for her phone number.

"I'm sorry," Clare said, as a roaming waiter appeared with a tray of pastry puffs, "but I'm here with my husband, Dr. Burt Wolf." She popped a puff in her mouth and smiled sweetly before walking away.

Dr. Burt Wolf. She pulled him out of the ether! He had been her imaginary friend when she was little. The real Dr. Burt Wolf was her mother's fiancé, in the early sixties, before Ruth met Mel. Clare must have heard the name when she was a child and picked up on some kind of emotional warp in the air.

"Why didn't you marry him?" Clare asked Ruth, not long ago.

"Well, Burt got a job offer at a very prominent radiology

department in *Baltimore,*" Ruth said. Even all these years later, she sounded weirdly proud of him. "Of course, I couldn't leave Oma and Opa, so I ended it."

"You . . . what?" The world was a kaleidoscope, its colors rearranging with the smallest twist.

Ruth shrugged. "I couldn't leave my parents, so I ended the engagement."

The weddings. All of the weddings. The seventh one was at a fancy hotel in downtown Chicago. Her high school friend Pete toasted his new wife with a catch in his voice. "I knew from the moment we met that we were meant to be, and nothing could ever keep us apart."

The guests raised their glasses in unison, and Clare took an extra long swallow of the lukewarm Champagne.

She met Matthew at a party. He was standing, pink-cheeked, in the middle of a crowded living room, and women fluttered around him like hummingbirds. "Oh, my God, your accent is *so charming,*" one of them said, and Clare rolled her eyes at the exact moment Matthew happened to glance over at her. Later, he told her, "You were so unimpressed. I wanted to impress you."

He was a journalist from England, here for only a year—already eight months into the year, in fact. ("Good Christ," he said, "your winter." As if she were personally responsible for it.) He was working on a master's degree in ecology. He wrote about climate change, the melting glaciers. Invasive mussels and the rising seas. "I'm a fun date," he said, laughing. But he was.

He had four months left in the city before he would earn his degree and go home. There was no harm in four months.

He said, "Will you go for a walk by the lake with me on Friday?" Other boys would say, "I don't know . . . what do you want to do?" or "Let's hang out sometime, get a beer or something, whatever," or, once, "Can you pay for my dinner?"

They met at the entrance to the park and picked their way down the stony path to the lake. A few minutes in, Matthew stumbled on a loose rock on the trail and began to slide. Scrabbling to catch himself, he grabbed Clare's arm.

He laughed nervously and stopped walking, held on to her arm for an extra second or two. "Shite, I'm sorry."

Clare said, "If you'd fallen, I would have gone down with you!"

"Yes," Matthew said. "That was intentional. I figured it's best you find that out now."

He was a few years older than Clare—probably in his early thirties. His hair was a little too long and he kept needing to brush it out of his eyes. She thought about standing very close to his face and gently taking a scissors to the shaggy edges of his hair. They started walking again, down the sloping path toward the shore.

"The lake is so beautiful and clear today," Clare said when they had reached the water. She picked up a flat stone and tried to skip it, a skill she had never mastered but always thought she might, similar to how she secretly suspected she might be psychic but it just hadn't surfaced yet. The rock fell into the lake with an inelegant splash.

"I have to tell you something," Matthew said. He turned to face her. The wind blew his hair out of his eyes. He squinted into the sun, took a deep breath. "The water is unnaturally clear because of zebra mussels, an invasive species that consumes plankton, which is a foundation of the Great Lakes food chain." He shook his head. "I'm sorry."

Clare laughed and chucked another stone into the sparkling water. "That's awful."

"I know. Occupational hazard."

There were other people on the beach, some teenagers

playing Frisbee, a group of little kids darting in and out of the water. Three girls on a beach towel rolled over in unison, like hot dogs in a 7-Eleven.

The magic trick of love is focus, the 20/20 vision of it. Matthew smiled at Clare and kicked off his shoes and took a step into the water, stretched out his hand, an invitation. She bent and untied her sneakers, peeled off her socks, and stuffed one in each shoe, carefully placed them out of reach of the lapping water. She waded in. The water was so cold she yelped; the cold shot up into her heart and paused the working machinery of her body.

"Nope!" she yelled, turning back to the sand. "No way! Abort mission!"

Matthew followed her out of the water. The bottoms of his jeans were sopping wet, indigo. "I thought you were a hearty native!"

They walked along the slim, smooth strand between the freezing lake and the slice of jagged rocks that lined the beach. They let the sun warm their feet.

Clare had been to nine weddings since she graduated from college seven years ago, six in the last year alone. She was a practical person, not prone to sentimentality. Still, the weight of it felt physical sometimes, like a density in her arms and legs, and—she couldn't help it—she wished she were lighter. She wished for the lilt and ease she saw in her friends but could never achieve for herself. She felt like a wax statue of *A Young Woman in Her Twenties,* or a very old woman with excellent skin.

They searched for sea glass and shells. Matthew caught an errant Frisbee, tossed it back. After a while they began the climb back up to the park's exit, and when they got to the parking lot Matthew said, "Can we go somewhere?"

So they drove back to her apartment. It was late afternoon. She poured them each a glass of water, then left the untouched glasses on her small kitchen table. They went into her bedroom and lay down on her bed. Neither of them was surprised; this was where the afternoon had been going, though she wondered, briefly, if all along she should have been protecting herself better.

But now Matthew's face was close to hers, warm breath and lips on her neck, and his hands were charting a map of her body.

She heard her mother's voice in her head: "Men don't buy the cow if they can get the milk for free!" Was she the cow in this scenario? Her mother's voice was always there, answering questions she hardly knew she was asking.

For once, she forced herself to silence it.

When she woke up, the only light was from the clock beside her bed, and for a second Clare didn't know what the breathing lump next to her was. When she remembered, a thrill flooded through her, a liquid mix of wanting and embarrassment.

The line between nothing and something was thread-thin. A moment of connection was compensation for the repetitive job of being alive. She knew this wasn't love. But she wondered, in the soft inky quiet, if it *could* be, if they might decide to turn it into that.

Her bedroom shades were up, the window open to the late-spring air. It was 9:30 p.m., and she was starving. She stretched and rearranged herself, trying to will Matthew awake, and then, because in her stretching she had kicked him, he did wake up. She could just make out the angle of his jaw, the curve of his shoulders. "Ow," he said. He was a face and a body and he rolled toward her in the dark.

He had a son in England. That was one of the first things he told her, on the beach that day. Nobody could accuse him of pretending to be something he wasn't, or of offering more of himself than he could give. The boy's name was Jack, he was four years old, and he lived with his mother, Matthew's ex, in a suburb outside of London.

"He's my magnet," Matthew said. "My home will always be London." A way of saying, "Let's not get too attached."

Jack loved soccer and had a cat, "a practically feral fucker," Matthew said. "He adores it." A look passed over his face, a little dreamy, stupid with love. "I really miss him."

"The cat?" Clare said.

Matthew laughed. "Yes."

His ex was an environmental scientist, he told her. They'd gotten together in college. *At university,* he said. Her name was Deirdre.

He had a son. She imagined a cherubic blond boy who called his mother "Mummy." Who called Matthew "Daddy."

Clare was silent for a few long seconds. "That's a hard name to say. Deirdre."

Matthew turned and looked at her, eyebrows raised. "I guess so, a little. Her friends call her Didi."

Did he still call her Didi? Did they have a secret language? Clare closed her eyes for a second and rearranged the puzzle she'd been putting together in her head. English Deirdre. She flashed on an image of Princess Diana in a lab coat, elegantly swirling murky lake water around in a beaker.

He told her about his family, too. His mother was Jewish. They'd celebrated Christmas and Hanukkah, he said.

"Oh! Lucky duck!" She was half serious. She'd had such Christmas envy growing up. "No contest!"

He nodded, a little sheepishly. "But it's different in England," he said. "I wanted to invite a friend for Passover one year, and my mum said, 'No, we're not zoo animals!'"

"Jesus!" Clare said.

He waited a beat. "Well, she might have let me bring him."

A gull winged and circled over the water and then dove. Nearby, a brown dog galloped down the edge of the water, a huge hunk of driftwood clamped in its mouth. They walked along the beach, and the sand that was adhering to their feet would transfer to her bed, would stay there for two weeks, grainy at the bottom, until she finally did laundry.

She had been bewitched, most likely. A spell had been cast on her body. Her skin fizzed as if fingers were lightly tracing over it even when she was alone, fully clothed, out in public.

Her body was an engine left idling. She was half of a secret.

How long could this possibly last?

She invited Matthew to her parents' house for dinner. "It's no big deal!" she told him, but she went over the day before to remove the picture of her as a naked two-year-old from the front hallway, to take down the sign her mother had hanging next to the refrigerator of a chubby pig scolding, A SECOND ON THE LIPS, A LIFETIME ON THE HIPS! She tucked her Most Improved Swimmer trophy into a drawer. Moved the three pairs of her mother's underwear that were draped over the shower rod like pennants.

The house you grew up in was your psyche's excretions, its sweat and its sneezes. It was the time you cut your own bangs in seventh grade, and the smell of your mother's tuna casserole that clung to your clothes. It was the House of Usher, no matter how well loved you were.

She and Matthew walked through the door. Her parents' elderly yellow Lab, Winifred, wandered over and licked her hello, sniffed Matthew, then farted and ambled off, toenails clicking on the granite tiles. Matthew squeezed Clare's hand, and the squeeze drew her free-floating anxiety right there into his sweaty palm and captured it.

"Thank you for having me over," Matthew said to Ruth, and Ruth, inscrutable, ushered them into the living room.

Mel was sitting on the couch, engrossed in a crossword puzzle. He looked up at them, surprised as a newborn chick, then stood up and hugged Clare and shook Matthew's hand, the tips of his fingers black with ink. "Forty-four down?" he said, and thrust the folded-up paper at her. Matthew peered over her shoulder. The clue was "Mediterranean building material."

She had brought boys home before—a college boyfriend, that med student. She understood now that they hadn't meant anything.

"Stucco!" Matthew said. Mel winked. He already knew that.

Ruth had made chicken Parmesan. As they sat down at the

table, Clare had the stunning realization—too late to save him!—that she and her father were so accustomed to her mother's bad cooking that they didn't notice it. Matthew took one bite of a chicken breast as dry as a sock, and his face registered a triptych of distress: surprise, panic, resignation. Clare almost choked on her water.

Matthew tried so hard to impress Ruth. Not Mel—there was no need for that. Mel was melting butter. Mel sensed another person's discomfort and met it with his own effusive goodwill, the secret handshake of the socially awkward. He recognized other people's nervousness and flipped over on his back to display his own pale underbelly. He was thrilled to show off his collection of vintage *MAD* magazines, his obscure jazz LPs, his novelty ties. He laughed at jokes that weren't funny because you *tried*.

But Ruth. She was ice.

Matthew tapped on her hard shell and set to work trying to crack it. He complimented the wallpaper and the crystal salad bowl and he finished every cotton-wool bite of that chicken Parmesan like an endurance athlete. He talked and talked, described his master's thesis in detail, held forth on warm Arctic winters and starving polar bears. He tried so hard a sweat broke out on his forehead. The whole time, there was a little dot of tomato sauce on his chin. Clare kept wiping her own chin to send him a clue, but he didn't read it.

She watched her mother evaluate him as if he were a cut of meat.

"Polar bears' long gestation period and low reproductive rate make them especially inadaptable to environmental change," Matthew said, though no one was really listening anymore. He nodded, then took a long sip of water.

A tiny piece of her snapped off. Clare saw him through Ruth's eyes now: his inability to read his audience, the way his eagerness to please slid into over-serious chatter. How he took a helping of salad for himself and forgot to pass the bowl around. His accent! It ramped up when he was trying to charm. She was almost sure of it.

A little spark of fury ignited in Clare, a purple flare of anger at her mother, or at Matthew, or at both of them.

Why couldn't she detach herself from the silent opinions of the separate human who happened to be her mother? What was wrong with her? She dug her nails into her palms and looked over at her father, who was, at that moment, staring lovingly at a slice of buttered bread.

Later, after Matthew had shaken Mel's hand and kissed Ruth on the cheek and was standing in the doorway, looking like he was waiting for a biopsy result, Ruth hugged Clare and brought her mouth to her ear and stage-whispered, "My goodness, he certainly cares about those polar bears, doesn't he?"

Clare felt it blow through her, that little wisp of nastiness, dank as a coil of fog from a frozen river. She knew what it meant. She knew what it would always mean. Whether it was polar bears, or a braying laugh, or any seed of love that threatened to grow in Clare's heart: "Don't go. He can't take you away from me."

I was in Bingen today visiting the cousins, and Hermann

asked why we don't sell the store. I don't know what to

do. I don't know what to do. . . .

Like an old married couple, Oskar and Walter can't agree on how their friendship began. The fact is that Oskar Beck's optometry clinic is two doors down from Goldmann's Shoes, but beyond that, the rest of the story changes every time they tell it.

"The first time I saw you, you were carrying a leaning tower of shoeboxes," Oskar says, his cheeks flushed from the wine. "You couldn't see over them. I had just unlocked my door when I saw you, and I thought, 'Who is this clown? He needs my help!'"

Walter stubs out his cigarette in the ashtray—a wedding gift from Oskar, as a matter of fact, a funny little green glazed earthenware dish comprised of two dogs sitting back to back, the hollow space between them perfect for resting a lit cigarette when a man needs both hands to illustrate his point. Every time Walter looks at it, he thinks fondly of his best friend. "You were not my knight in shining armor!" he says. "Although it's true I couldn't see a thing. You came up behind me like a cat burglar. I thought you were trying to steal those boxes!" They laugh together, and Walter extends his arm to Annelise, who is nearby, clearing the dinner dishes. She comes close, still holding an unused cloth napkin, and he wraps his arm around her waist and draws her in. She relaxes into his embrace for a second, then returns to the table, blushing, pleased. This kind of pleasure—warm and physical, inattentive to worry, concerned only with the goodness of the moment—has grown so rare.

Oskar has been coming over for dinner once a week, sometimes twice, practically since she and Walter got married—always with a bottle of Riesling and flowers or candy for her, a kiss on the hand, a gallant little bow, then an eager, pumping handshake with Walter. Annelise looks forward to his visits more than she cares to admit.

In the very beginning, he was such a pleasing addition to their life, the perfect offshoot of her domestic certainty: at the table of their marital happiness, she and Walter showed Oskar an ideal to strive for (she thought), and he, in his bachelorhood, brought them shiny glimpses of the outside world, funny stories about the girls he took out on dates, young women from the synagogue his mother wanted him to meet and then—within minutes, it seemed—marry. He was their project, a pet.

But lately Oskar has been simmering with fury. Lately he talks about leaving more than anything else.

Walter and Annelise are still trying to remain optimistic: even as they say good-bye to people (their neighbors the Siegels in July; her dear Emmi and Emmi's husband and baby girl, just last month). This past September, when their citizenship was revoked—even reeling from that blow, they're trying. But Oskar rages now, constantly, and Walter is beginning to respond to it, sizzling and sparking like a live wire.

"They won't stop," Oskar announced over dinner last week. "They'll keep taking," he said, "until we have nothing left!" And Walter gripped the arms of his chair and said nothing.

Annelise took Oskar aside a few weeks ago. "We're not going anywhere," she told him. "Not yet. So, please."

She spent all afternoon baking mohnkuchen for tonight's dessert. It's a labor of love, this cake—the crust demanding orange zest (when oranges are hard to come by) and a light touch, and you have to beat the egg whites at the precise moment you're ready to use them for both the topping and the filling, which means you have to grow two extra hands to get it just right. And as if that's not enough, you're left, afterward, with sticky little poppy seeds scattered over every kitchen surface like an infestation of tiny black bugs.

She's tidying up in the kitchen now, washing dishes, wiping down the countertops, sweeping. (Good grief, is her mother right? These labors *are* soothing!) Walter and Oskar are still talking in the dining room, their low voices rumbling into the kitchen like new thunder. She's absorbed in the cleanup when she hears a loud thump and the rattle of cups and saucers—a fist come down hard on a table.

Annelise freezes, her hands suspended in lukewarm soapy water. After few seconds, the door to their apartment slams shut, and she dries her hands and rushes back into the sitting room.

Oskar is standing alone, near the window. The air in the room feels strange and still, as if lightning has just struck. "Your husband stepped outside for a cigarette," Oskar says, and he raises his eyebrows at her as if they're in on a wry little joke together. Most of the mohnkuchen sits untouched on its platter, and a bony little finger of irritation scratches at her. The violence in the streets is an abomination. She is afraid every day! But this is her home. Here, now, in this still and fragile moment, she has the right to ignore the menace, or, if not ignore, then to regard it, with the alert pose of a small mammal, as a threat that might still pass. Men will never allow you to sustain the peace that you have so carefully created!

Annelise gathers the last of the plates from the table and moves past Oskar. He taps her shoulder to stop her and lifts the stack of dishes from her hands. She sighs. "Please," he says, "let me," and he follows her into the kitchen.

Oskar stands next to her at the sink. Steam rises from the basin. She washes and he dries. They are, for these moments, a silent and efficient economy. Their bodies are close, almost touching as she hands him a wet plate and he takes it, as he reaches toward her while she dips a cup into the tub of clean water. He's warm, from the summer air or the whiskey. His fingertips, she notices, are clean, unstained. (Walter's are yellowish, no matter how much he washes them.) Sensitive to the smell of tobacco on the hands and the intimacy of his profession, Oskar is not a smoker.

You married one man. But life is really an array of unchosen options, isn't it? Of open doors clicked closed or slammed shut, or doors that have never been open, not even a crack, and will stay that way forever. Life is lived in pairs, eyes straight ahead and carefully choreographed movements, but all you have to do is turn your head slightly, and you can see it all.

"Lise," Oskar says, as he wipes the last plate. Her own name sounds odd to her. She thinks that maybe Oskar has never actually said it before. He clears his throat. "This is going to be very bad. For all of us." Lifted from her little reverie, it takes her a moment to understand what he's saying.

She shrugs, echoes her father, her husband: "These things

always pass." Her voice sounds girlish and trivial to her own ears.

Oskar slides the last plate into the cupboard. "They want us gone."

She takes the cloth he was holding and wipes her hands on it, looks at his face. He's shorter than Walter, only a few inches taller than she is. There's that tug of annoyance again, but this time it feels desperate, hotter. With whom do you align yourself? Maybe you won't know until it's too late. Maybe you'll never know.

Annelise turns away from Oskar and hangs the damp towel on a hook above the sink. She is unsurprised to feel his palm on her back tracing lightly down to the bow of her dress at the base of her spine. She shivers.

But no. Oskar is nowhere near her. He has already moved away from her, is sitting, now, at the kitchen table. The hand on her back was her imagination.

The front door creaks open, and Walter comes back into the kitchen. The sharp, familiar smell of tobacco lingers on him. She hears him pull out a chair, sit down with a thud. Annelise is still at the sink, draining the basin. She keeps her back to them deliberately—flushed, bothered.

"The optometrist thinks he can see the future," Walter says, and Annelise tenses, but she turns, finally, and sees that he is grinning. There is no menace. The argument that brought his fist down onto the table is over now.

I live constantly in my thoughts with you.

She wakes up in the darkness, knowing. She has, of course, been told what to expect, but that doesn't matter. The pain wraps around her like a choking vine ("a pain," her mother said, "you can't fathom and will soon forget"). She nudges Walter awake, and he's out of bed and buttoning his shirt practically before she finishes her sentence.

There are so many reasons to leave.

Everyday terror, making itself as comfortable as a house-guest. The neighbors who won't speak to her, won't even look at her—and the one who does look at her, who glares at her as if he wants her dead, his lip curled in a sneer, the one with the strange child. Customers shunning the bakery, the business barely afloat. Whispers of arrests, homes ransacked. Police on the street, ugly graffiti, stores that will not allow her through the door. This breathless fog of hate.

But. The field behind the school where they played one-two-three-stop and cat-and-mouse. She would like to watch her son or daughter run in that field. The cobbled street outside their apartment, her feet anticipating every wobbly stone. The fall festival they provided pastries for every year—well, no longer—but memories of it, wine and beer and laughing neighbors. Mrs. Brandt, who altered her dresses. Mr.

Schulte, who hated children. Mrs. Engel, her mother's friend, who gave them apples from her tree. The robins—generations of them, she figures—who visited her windowsill every spring. Detail after detail after detail, her life.

At the hospital, they give her medicine that the nurse promises will ease the pain, but it doesn't work. She feels everything. Every vise-crush, every searing rip. It's formless, unbearable. She smells the iron-sharp scent of her own blood. She wants her mother.

Later—minutes? hours?—Klara is there, gazing down at the swaddled infant in her arms. The baby bleats like a tiny goat. Annelise, through her exhaustion, sees her mother's face above her, radiant in the blurry light.

Klara leans forward and adjusts the baby in Annelise's arms. "Oh, look," she says, to Annelise, to the child, to herself. "Look."

The thought of going rises, recedes, rises.

What is she supposed to do now? What can she possibly do now?

When Annelise lost the first baby, Walter phoned Klara and Julius to break the news. The doctor had been to see her, Walter told Klara, and Annelise was resting. "I'm sorry," he said. "Nothing could be done." And then, again, as if he'd forgotten he'd just said it: "I'm sorry."

A little moan escaped her before she clamped her mouth shut. In the silence on the other end of the line, Walter waited, then said, "Klara, are you there?"

As a young woman, she had not dreamed of a large family. Julius wanted four or five children, but to Klara that sounded like bedlam! She pretended to agree with him, but secretly she planned on only two: a girl and a boy. She imagined miniature replicas of herself and Julius, a tidy family, even-numbered and orderly. She had always been partial to even numbers.

Naturally, she'd hoped to become pregnant as soon as they were married, to get down to the business of raising a family. Six months passed, eight months, ten. Hope trickled like a slow leak. Four years, and she was desolate. Julius was kind, but the failure was hers, and her pain was hot and private.

And then, wondrous and disorienting as a dream, came Annelise. The first and the last.

Now, finally, Ruthie: the perfect answer to a question she's been asking for almost twenty-five years.

Most Sunday afternoons, Annelise leaves the baby with

Klara. Klara lives for those hours, cleans and tidies before-
hand as if she's preparing the apartment for royalty. Julius
teases her about it—*When will our princess be here?*—but that's
exactly what she thinks, and she does not care to take any
chances with germs.

Of course, she would love nothing more than to bundle
Ruthie up and parade her around Feldenheim, but that's
impossible now. She won't do it. Mr. and Mrs. Ziegler, their
neighbors for twenty-six years, hung their giant flag in their
street-facing window, and another, smaller one in the courtyard window—the one that only residents of the building can
see. Irma Ziegler had the nerve to clutch her arm in passing
a few weeks ago and whisper, "We've never had any problem
with you." Klara shook her head and hurried on.

Every week, she notices something else about the baby: a
slightly different expression on her face, a knowingness in her
eyes; the way her lips practice forming different shapes, a prelude to words. One week, a little more dark hair on her head.
The next, she could swear those little potato feet are slightly
longer, slimmer.

Last week, they were required to give up their typewriter.
They received official notice to bring it to the police station—
the black typewriter in the back office where they tallied their
receipts, clacking background noise to their bookkeeping,
a necessary object they didn't even think about until it was
taken from them. Hands shaking, Klara pulled the last sheet
of paper from the roller, the bakery's weekly ledger. Julius carried the typewriter to the station, holding it in front of him,
his head down. Another wedge of their dignity.

So, no, Klara would not leave the house with Ruthie.

Annelise has left, and Julius is at the bakery now, getting the store ready for tomorrow. She and Ruthie are alone, which is what Klara loves best—the two of them, rapt and attentive to each other, a perfect little exchange between need and fulfillment.

She's holding Ruthie on her hip, walking around the living room and singing a nonsensical tune about dogs, when Ruthie frowns in concentration and releases a series of indelicate grunts.

"That's all right," Klara says, although the baby does not look apologetic. "We'll take care of that, won't we?" She kisses Ruthie on the nose and scans the room for the carrying bag Annelise always leaves with her, a little leather satchel full of extra diapers, glass bottles, a rag doll, a change of clothing. "We'll just clean you right up," Klara says, but she can't find the bag.

She walks around the apartment, still holding Ruthie, searching all of the places Annelise might have left it. Did she go into the kitchen when Klara was distracted by the baby? Did she leave the bag on the crisply made bed in her old bedroom, the room, Klara imagines, where Ruthie will one day stay on overnight visits when she's older, snuggling under the down comforter that once belonged to Annelise? She shifts the baby and pulls her close, despite the increasingly unpleasant odor.

If only Annelise thought before she acted, if only she weren't so scattered, so . . . birdbrained! Klara feels the old scrape of irritation, that hot ember in her chest. She considers her options. There is a limited amount of time before this little cleanup job will require a full bath. She has none of the necessary items here. Annelise and Walter live just four blocks away. It's the beginning of April, cool and sunny.

Ruthie is babbling happily in her arms now, but soon it will be too late to prevent a rash. Not to mention, soon she will be hungry, and Klara has milk but no bottles. Everything she needs is in that bag. She has to go. She'll go. She finds her coat, pulls a small wool blanket from the linen closet, and wraps it snugly around the baby. Fueled by her vexation, she leaves the apartment, locks the door behind her, walks with purpose down the hall and out the building's main door.

The sunlight is gorgeous on her face, almost liquid. She breathes in deeply, begins to make her way down the block. It's Sunday, quiet. Hardly anyone is out, not her neighbors, not the thugs, not the thugs who are her neighbors. She holds Ruthie tightly; the bounce of Klara's quick step is already lulling her. "Sweet baby," she murmurs. Ruthie's eyelids flutter.

She is a woman walking down the street of the small city where she has lived her entire adult life. She belongs here, carrying her grandchild, the sun on her face. She walks at a clip past the homes of people she knows and people she might know: women who sigh and pick up the dirty socks their husbands have left on the floor by the side of the bed; young wives who worry they don't know what they're doing; children who squabble, whose mothers snap, *"Stop it"*; elderly couples who drink tea in the morning, hardly talking.

Ruthie wakes up with a start, looks up at Klara, registers surprise. Klara holds her tightly, her arms starting to ache a bit. What she feels for this baby is almost like pain, an exquisite stinging behind her eyes. She has so, so much to be grateful for. These dark days won't last. She's been around long enough to have seen the way opinions ebb and flow. She looks around her, alert to everything, anticipating movement. She slows her pace a bit.

One more block and she'll be at Annelise's doorstep. She can see their building from here. Her irritation has mostly subsided, but, she thinks, she will still share with her daughter the effects of the girl's forgetfulness. Lise is so young, still learning! *Do you see?* Klara will say, handing her the baby. *If you had simply planned ahead, had thought in advance about what you needed to do, made a list, one-two-three. If you had just anticipated the needs of others.*

She's almost there. The early spring wind is bracing. Flags snap in the breeze. A young man walks toward her. She didn't notice him, and now he's a few feet in front of her, and it's too late to cross the street. Her heart hammers. She glances up as they pass each other, just in time to see him glaring at her, his mouth a grim and lipless line. With a jolt, she knows what he sees. She feels his disdain like a knife, quick and lacerating. Ruthie opens her mouth like a little fish, blows a tiny bubble of saliva. Breathe, now. She reminds herself to breathe.

Annelise rushes to the door at the first loud knock. She's been reading (a guilty pleasure—dinner isn't made; the apartment is a mess), and when she hears the urgent rapping, she slips her novel under a couch pillow and runs to open the door. She takes one look at her mother and gasps, pulls her inside.

"You forgot the baby's bag!" Klara says, voice high and brittle. "She soiled herself, Lise, and I didn't know what else to do!" Ruthie claps with joy at the sight of her mother.

"Mama!" Annelise says, breathing in her mother's fear (and a whiff of the baby, too). The bag? No, but she . . . well, maybe? Her own certain memory collides with her mother's accusation, submits to it. Lise takes Ruthie, her mother's coat, the baby's blanket. "Come." She guides her mother to the kitchen table. "I'll take care of Ruthie and then I'll make you tea."

Klara lets herself be led, sits, grasps the edge of the table with both hands. Annelise carries Ruthie into the other room and sings to her as she changes her diaper. A few minutes later, she brings the talcum powder–scented baby back into the kitchen, hands her over again to Klara. *That child's feet will never touch the floor,* Julius likes to tease.

Annelise puts on the kettle. She's off-kilter now, thrown by this unexpected interruption, by her mother's panic. There will be no coming back from it, she thinks, with a sudden, astringent clarity. Even if everything returned to normal with a snap of her fingers, even if the rot cleared out today, this minute, life will never be the way it once was. She finishes preparing the tea, glad for the few moments at the stove.

She sets two cups and matching saucers on the table—from her wedding set, bluebells on white porcelain; it makes her happy just to look at them. She pours the tea, then pulls out a chair for herself and sits down.

"Fresh and clean," Klara says, bending to kiss the baby's head.

Annelise feels an odd blend of regret and relief as she watches her mother and daughter together. She has never really known how to talk to Klara. Ruthie is their new language.

The baby wiggles on Klara's lap, claps again, and demonstrates her latest skill—very happy, very loud yelping.

"Good lungs," Klara says, over the squawks.

"What?" Lise asks.

"*Lungs,*" I said. *"Good lungs!"*

Ruthie crows even more insistently, drowning out Klara and Lise completely, and the two women give up, laughing.

Later, in the dimming light, Walter will walk Klara home. They'll hurry, silent, through the streets as the spring sky fades into violet.

Even later, Klara will find the baby's bag stashed neatly in the front closet. There it is. How did she not see it? She'll remove the items, one by one, and lay them out: diapers, washcloth, small tin of talcum powder, soft yellow blanket, glass bottles, rag doll. Nothing missing, neatly organized. All there.

Walter, like all shopkeepers, has an uncanny sense of time. He knows that it's 11:00 when the browsing ladies begin to trickle in (eager to be convinced, perhaps a pretty Spanish heel?). It's somewhere between 3:40 and 4:00 when the housewives finishing up their afternoon errands bustle through (practical shoppers; show them this season's lace-up Oxford). Five o-clock is the hour of the demanding madam. She will take her sweet time. There goes your dinner.

Well, that's how it used to be. Business is terrible now. But he still knows when it's time to close the store—not by the angle of the light or the tick of his wristwatch, but by his own internal mechanics. Tonight he begins the ritual as the white February moon is high in the sky. Cold wind rattles the front window. Time to box up the display shoes and lower the awning, although he is tempted to stay open a bit longer on the off-chance a customer might wander in. But Lise and the baby are waiting for him at home, and all he can think about is seeing their faces.

He's sent Erich home and is running the carpet sweeper over the rugs when someone raps on the window. He squints into the darkness and can just make out a tall figure—a familiar slouch, a particular curve of the shoulders. He feels an acidic sluice of love and disappointment, sweetness and dismay: recognition lands in his stomach before it registers in his brain. He nods curtly, locks the front door, then walks to the back of the store and through the stockroom to let his old friend inside. It's been two years.

Walter is not a man who allows his emotions to run rough-shod over him. That kind of indulgence is for artists, musicians, women. So he is surprised to note that his hand shakes just a little bit as he undoes the chain from the back door, that his mouth is dry, his breathing shallow. What does Ernst want with him? Can things have fallen so far that he is here to make trouble?

Walter steps aside as Ernst rushes in, accompanied by a blast of air. Ernst glances around, looks at Walter, his face a question.

"It's all right," Walter says. "I've locked up. It's just us."

Ernst stomps his feet on the floor, rubs his hands together. The cold steams off him. He's wrapped in a gray overcoat, which he opens dramatically, like a flasher, to reveal a bottle of kirschwasser tucked into the lining. He grins at Walter and waggles his eyebrows. As if no time has passed.

"Remember?" Ernst says, and Walter wants to say, "No," and, "What are you talking about?" and, "Get the hell out of my store," but of course he does, he remembers, and he bites down hard on the inside of his cheek.

They used to pilfer this very same schnapps from Ernst's father's liquor cabinet, and despite Walter's best efforts to repress it, he can feel it even now, standing here in the stock-room: the two of them, fourteen years old in Ernst's father's study, hearts pounding, thrilled with themselves and terrified, alert to heavy footsteps. Straight from the bottle, first Ernst, then Walter. The gulp of alcohol fiery down his throat, bitter almond lingering on his tongue.

Walter clears a space for the bottle on his cluttered desk and motions for Ernst to sit down. Walter reaches behind the desk, finds two dusty, mismatched glasses, wipes the insides with a clean shoe cloth. Ernst pours—generously, as always—then throws back a shot. Walter takes small, suspicious sips. Everything about Ernst is familiar, even the way he smells, everything except his enthusiastic membership in the Nazi party. Walter will not lose himself to this moment.

"How is your lovely wife?" Ernst asks.

Walter looks at him, doesn't answer. He has the sudden, unwelcome image of Ernst as a young boy. His mother would shave his head every September, in case he caught head lice, which he usually managed to do anyway. For the first few weeks of school Ernst had the look of a baby bird, soft blond tufts all over his skull. You can't look at a person you've known since childhood without seeing all of him, the sediment of years.

Ernst wipes a little bead of water from the tip of his nose and pours himself another glass of kirschwasser. "How is your wife?" he asks again.

"Fine," Walter says. Ernst joined the party long before there was any pressure to do so. He's a true believer. "She's fine." Walter doesn't want to give his old friend anything, not an ounce of himself, not a speck. He stares at his glass, at the clear liquid innocent as water.

"Suit yourself," Ernst says, shrugging. "I'll get right to it." He runs the palm of his left hand over his cheek and then peers around the stockroom again. Ernst is pale, Walter notices, and his voice is pitched several decibels lower than the boisterous boom he remembers.

Walter swallows another sip, waits a beat. "What is it?" But he knows.

"Your name has come up. They're going to accuse you of being a communist." He puts his glass down, picks it up. Nervous. "You have to go."

His name. Walter feels something crawl across his skin, a beetling skitter. He still believes that his name belongs to him, that the way he lives his life—above reproach—is his protection. He shakes his head. "My business," he says.

"Soon you won't have a business." Ernst sets his glass down on the desk again, sighs. "What will convince you, my friend? They'll take you from your family. Your wife, your child."

So many people have already left. But hasn't that just been so much panic? Doesn't he pride himself on being reasonable? "I'm not a communist," he says. He gestures with his empty glass to the stockroom, as if his shoe store proves that, proves anything.

Ernst tilts his head, looks at Walter with genuine surprise. "You're not a communist, but you are a Jew and also an idiot. They should arrest you for being an idiot." He laughs at his own joke. Still Ernst.

For the first time, right here, in the cluttered stockroom of his store, surrounded by boxes of shoes, order sheets, deliveries, an apple and a half-eaten sandwich and an emptying bottle of kirschwasser and his childhood friend, he sees that none of it will protect him. He can practically feel the silt falling from his eyes as his head lifts from the sand. He'll owe this to Ernst forever.

"Walter," Ernst says. "Do you hear me? I'm telling you something. You have to make your preparations. You have to get your affairs in order."

Walter is a little bit drunk, he realizes. Dizzy, his head buzzing. Ernst could always hold his liquor better than he could.

"You need to leave," Ernst says.

And then Ernst, friend of his youth, swallows one more shot of kirschwasser and does.

About that table.

Naturally, they discarded the brick that shattered the window, flew across the dining room, and crashed into their table, splintering off a corner of it. But they kept the table.

Afterward, Annelise wanted to smash the top with a hammer and burn the legs, but Walter insisted they keep the table that bore the horrible scar of the brick that was meant to destroy them—their peace, their home, their lives. Why? Annelise wondered, a scream in her head for days, and for God's sake, who? But there was no explanation beyond the obvious one: they were hated.

In fact, that beautiful mahogany table will come with them on the ship to America, and it will sit in the dining rooms of their succession of small apartments (so much smaller than their apartment in Feldenheim; in their first tiny flat, it crowds the room so tightly there is hardly room to sit).

"We'll never get it fixed," Walter says. "Every day, it will remind us that we did what we had to do."

But every day of her life Annelise sets this table, drapes a blue cloth over the gash, and all she sees is what she lost: not the people she loved—she thinks about them plenty without any sort of reminder—but the things, the things. She can never admit it, having escaped with their lives, can never admit how much it hurts to lose so many nice things: the feel of a beautiful blue and gold Oriental rug beneath bare feet, the soft pink glow from the Tiffany lamp, her silver tea service, the leaded stained glass in the window above the staircase that scattered sunlight into prisms.

What kind of person mourns *things* when so many of her dear ones are ashes?

So Walter was right. That table is a reminder, but not in the way he thought. It's the spoiled, clawing fury of wanting everything back the way it was. It's the humiliation that lives outside her heart. Every time she passes it, on her way from the kitchen to the bedroom, the living room to the bathroom, her desire to scream is undiminished.

An undented table, its perfection a lie, its surface an illusion, is a smooth, easy pleasure. What she wouldn't give for such a thing.

If I only had your stockings here to mend. I'm sure you don't have much time to do it.

———

There was nothing this baby couldn't heal. Klara felt it from the first time she held Ruthie. Her grandchild, her only: dark curls matted to her warm forehead in yeasty sleep, pink cheeks, perfect lips pursed, whistling softly as she exhaled, slack in Klara's arms. She would have sat rocking the child all night if she could have. To hold her was both longing and the satisfaction of that very longing in one full-to-bursting moment. Klara could feel the goodness of the whole world in that warm, breathing child.

She has done everything to the best of her limited abilities. She has made her share of mistakes, but she believes that she has been, on balance, a loving wife, a good mother. She has obeyed every rule.

She can't think too much about the good-bye. She can't let her mind touch down on it, those last moments at the train station, bright lights and the heaving crowd; everyone, it seemed, sobbing and clutching one another, and she herself stunned, dumbfounded, gasping.

All those days when she craved nothing more than a moment to sit quietly, weeks when it seemed she would never get her work done, years that flew past her in a hard gust of wind: all she wanted in that chaos was ten minutes to herself. And now that the children have left, and the bakery no longer belongs to them, she has so much time. She is marooned on an island of time.

Columns of sunlight shot through the windows of the domed train station, bouncing around the huge building. She crouched low in the midst of the crowd and wrapped Ruthie in her arms, tried to stay calm so as not to scare her. Her hands on Ruthie's little back, her face in her hair. The navy-blue high-collared, boiled wool coat she had bought for her. The apple-sweet smell of her. Every single second of Klara's life had borne her relentlessly into this one. Ruthie squirmed a little, then settled her cheek onto her grandmother's shoulder. Klara held her as the lower halves of bodies moved past them, legs and feet, legs and feet.

After a while, three or four minutes, Walter bent down and eased Ruthie from Klara's arms, and Julius pulled her up. "Come," he said softly, his mouth next to her ear.

For a flash, for just that broken moment, she despised both men. Her throat clogged. She couldn't swallow. A wild "no" formed in her chest and writhed through her. Her husband put his arm around her very gently, turned her away from her children, and led her away. Her legs buckled. She regained her balance.

She sits in a rocking chair in a darkening room, mending a rip in Julius's pants, trying to recall that breathing weight in her arms, trying to find comfort where there is none.

The little family had to leave. There was no doubt about that. When Ernst, Walter's best friend (and eager member of the SS; how does Walter reconcile that? He has always been too forgiving), whispered that they were going to accuse Walter of being a communist, it was the beginning of the end. Walter! A communist! Like accusing a bird of being a fish . . . no, of being a potato, a loaf of bread, a box. The thugs were going to come for him, and the children had no choice but to make their preparations.

Klara and Julius caught their train back to Feldenheim, rode home in silence. It was still early when they got back; the morning was brilliant and bright. They walked through the door of their apartment. Klara staggered down the hallway to her bedroom. Without taking off her coat, her shoes, she fell onto her bed. She lay there, awake and immobile, for hours. The clean smell of cotton mingled with her own souring breath. Julius brought her a bowl of noodle soup, which turned lukewarm and then stone cold on the table beside her. She didn't get up until late the next evening.

She finishes the sewing, loops a tiny, practiced knot, and bites off the last bit of thread. Once upon a time, there was a bottomless pile of mending: socks and stockings with holes where big toes had poked through, shirts with soft, threadbare patches at the elbows. Now there is just this one pair of pants, and that's done. She lets it fall across her lap like a blanket.

She closes her eyes, squeezes them shut until she sees flashing colors. She hears Julius making tea in the kitchen: the whistle of the kettle, the clink of two cups.

She imagines him walking toward her with the tea, and she waves her hand in front of her, shooing him away, although in fact he is still in the kitchen preparing it. "No," she whispers to herself.

She will focus her formidable energy, narrow as a blinding beam, on the project of leaving, so that she does not stay here, in this rocking chair, lost in memories, as her bones turn to dust.

If only I could see her for five minutes. I have always imagined how she looked with her curly hair.

Annelise opens her eyes on a Monday morning in the town she will forever, despite everything, think of as home. She pushes the covers aside without a sound, so that Ruthie and Walter can sleep for a few more minutes, so that she might have these last few moments alone with her parents. She sets her feet down lightly on the cool floor of her childhood bedroom in her parents' apartment and tiptoes into the kitchen to greet them: her mother, making coffee, and her father, sitting at the table, stricken. She notices the way the sun beams in through one window and lands on a corner of the red tablecloth, lighting a triangle of color on fire. She sits down across from her father and forces herself to sip the coffee her mother handed to her. Although her throat is thick and closed, she makes herself chew and swallow a fresh slice of buttered bread, and she can't stop herself from wondering how long it will be before she tastes bread her father has baked again. They sit together, the three of them, in silence, having said everything the night before.

Section Two

Her parents' basement smelled like old newspapers and air freshener—sweet decay with a top note of pine. In increments, Clare was helping them clean it. Once a week she would come over, have dinner, then head downstairs into the time warp. The process transported her directly back to her childhood: this imploding mountain of boxes was her grandparents' apartment, piled in the middle of the room. Here was their whole life in things, the sentimental and the practical, treasures rubbing elbows with trash: her grandmother's cylindrical aluminum cookie press, a Tiffany lamp, Clare's favorite plates (the white ones with the beautiful pink-cabbage-rose border). Old, water-stained cookbooks with Annelise's notations in the margins in German, glass jars of ancient spices and brass candlesticks from Germany and one entire box filled with Annelise's purses.

Clare and Ruth had packed up the apartment right after Annelise died, but they had paid no attention to detail. It was too soon for it. So they just threw everything into boxes. After they'd sold the furniture (and paid some teenagers to haul that splintered dining room table out to the curb), they really had only four carloads of things to transport to Ruth and Mel's, up and down the stairs to the basement ten, twenty, thirty times, and done.

The boxes stayed that way in the basement for a long time, unopened and ignored.

"Not yet," Ruth said, again and again. "Maybe in a month or two." Annelise was eighty-five when she died. Ruth was sixty-one. No matter. She grieved for her mother audaciously, like a child.

Finally one Sunday afternoon Clare went downstairs by herself. She tugged her hair into a ponytail, threw an old white T-shirt of her father's over her clothes. She was glad for the distraction.

She found an open packet of cherry cough drops in a white patent-leather purse, the top lozenge exposed and covered in lint, and she tucked the roll into her own pocket. She found a photo album, pictures of her mother as a toddler, round-cheeked and tiny, her mouth a tricky smile, as if she had just concocted a foolproof plan to rob a bank. She found a blue and white coffee grinder, the one she hardly noticed on her grandparents' kitchen wall all those years. She pried open the metal lid. Rough grounds and oily coffee bean casings dotted the bottom of the container. She breathed in the still-strong smell, the residue of her grandparents' lives—all that they had touched, consumed, discarded.

Clare was wrestling with a wobbly old floor lamp, winding its cord around the base and waltzing it over to the "discard" pile when she started at nothing—a ghost, a sixth sense—and glanced up.

Ruth was standing in the doorway. How long had she been there, silently surveying the room? She had one hand planted firmly on her hip and was clutching a tube of Colgate in the other. She smiled and waved the toothpaste at Clare like she was conducting an orchestra. "Sweetie," she said. "You can have this."

Clare swiped at her forehead with the back of her hand. "No, thanks, Mom. I don't want it."

"I got it with double coupons. But it's not the kind Dad and I like," she said. She stared at the pile of dresses on the floor, winter wools and summer linens, and Clare's eyes followed her mother's.

Annelise had been a very short woman, just shy of five feet tall. Clare shot past her by the time she was in fourth grade. She had favored pastels and thin belts, though she was short-waisted. She wore low heels and a full face of makeup to walk a half-block to the mailbox. And those purses. Clare had stacked them in a heap next to the dresses. It looked as if Annelise had just left the room after rampaging through her closet and finding everything unsuitable.

"I thought we could donate all of this to the high school's drama department, if that's okay," Clare said gently. "Don't you think that would be nice? For the clothes to have a second life like that?"

Ruth nodded. "I suppose so. Sure."

There was a framed painting of irises leaning against the wall. An empty yellow plastic garbage can and a table lamp. A green ashtray: two dogs, sitting back to back, with the space in the middle for cigarette butts. Where did that come from, and who had use for an ashtray these days?

"Dad and I won't even use this toothpaste," her mother said, coming back to herself. "You should just take it."

Clare allowed herself to roll her eyes at her mother, a pleasure reserved for special occasions now that she was actually an adult. "I don't need any toothpaste," she said, tapping on the lampshade to bring the point home.

She knew what Ruth was thinking: that Clare didn't *know* what she needed. That she had a job but no career, no husband, not even a nice boyfriend, just a lot of books in a tiny, dingy apartment in a not sufficiently safe neighborhood.

Her mother sighed. "Fine, don't take the toothpaste."

That sigh! It was Kryptonite to Clare. It was the heat that baked guilt right into her bones.

"All right," Clare said, steadying the broken lamp and walking over to her mother. "Okay. I will take the toothpaste."

Ruth shook her head. "No, don't if you don't want it."

"I want the toothpaste." Clare chewed the inside of her cheek. "I do."

"Hmm."

"Mom. Please. I would really like that toothpaste."

Her mother's face eased into a smile. "Good! I was hoping you would!"

Someone had to find them. How else would they be here, telling their mundane and anguished story?

Clare held the translucent paper in her hands and bits of it flaked off, vegetal fragments, and she thought, *Oh, that's why they call it onionskin.* She was their unlikely curator, reluctant beneficiary.

She brought them up close to her face. They smelled earthy and sweet, like dirt. They were something. Holding them like that, she couldn't know what: a fragile secret, a story. An explanation.

From the blankness of their vanished years and through their powdery teeth, the dead rose up and made themselves heard.

They lodged inside her like an instruction manual, specific and urgent.

What to do in case of emergency: Run fast. Seek safety.

But the directions didn't reach far enough into the future. What about when safety was found? When years and danger had passed, and a family, though small, was whole? What then?

Even though we haven't heard from you in three weeks, I will nevertheless write a few lines to you and report what's happening with us.

In my last letters I repeatedly asked, at different times, why you don't just put the letters next to you as you write, and then you can answer all of our questions.

You forgot your travel blanket. If I don't think of everything, that's what happens.

Does she still think about us?

Klara was real. She was prickly, desperate. Furious. Lost.

Clare, her namesake, lived ordinary days. A stack of novels wobbled on her nightstand. There were two bags of spinach in her refrigerator, a half-gallon of soy milk, and some questionable grapes. Seven boxes of cereal in the pantry, ice cream in the freezer. Her favorite blue glass bowl in the center of her little round kitchen table refracted the morning sunlight. She came home after work to the blinking light of her answering machine: "Sweetheart, it's Mom. Just calling to say hi."

Without telling her mother, who was too sad for it, Clare paid to have the letters translated. The translator mailed them back to her in a thick envelope. She sat on the lumpy green futon couch in her little apartment on a Sunday and read them, start to finish, 1938 to 1941.

The day passed, long light to purple dusk to dark. When she looked up, her coffee was cold, and she saw her own living room reflected in the window. She looked around and was surprised to be alone.

She loved living by herself, knowing that the way she left the apartment in the morning would be the same way she found it in the evening: her slippers in the hallway, robe hanging on the bathroom hook, small bag of licorice on the kitchen counter. She loved waking up on a weekend morning in her quiet bedroom, coming into her thoughts slowly, beholden to no one.

There was a softness to her life. But there was also a quietly pulsing heartache, sad and mystifying, a constant companion.

Did the letters answer a looming question she didn't know she had, or were they an excuse, psychic landfill?

They were scraps of someone she couldn't have known, a woman who died twenty-eight years before Clare was born. But Klara was familiar, familial. Clare heard her voice in the clutch of her own childhood, the engulfing worry, the protective spells.

But maybe that was just life.

A siren screamed past her apartment building. A man on the street below yelled something, and a woman called back to him, a greeting or possibly an obscenity. A dog barked.

She was porous. Her skin was the thinnest scrim between her delicate, pulpy self and the world with its sharp teeth.

She got up and closed the curtains, then sat back down on the futon. The overhead light was on, although she didn't remember flicking the switch. One of her neighbors was cooking a garlicky dinner. She remembered that she was almost out of shampoo.

She wasn't sure what to do next. She looked around at all of her comforting objects and understood that they were not anchors.

The translated letters, a one-sided lament, lay in a neat pile next to her.

*

She gave the letters to her mother and then, for two weeks, Ruth didn't mention them, not once. Finally, on the phone one night, Clare said, "Mom, aren't you going to read them?"

"Well," Ruth said, chewing, "I haven't had time."

"What are you eating?" It sounded like raw carrots. "Please stop chewing in my ear." Clare took a bite of her own pretzel, but she chewed very softly. "And what do you mean, you haven't had time?"

"Almonds. And I mean I haven't had time." She munched, irritatingly. "Your father needs new glasses."

Clare closed her eyes.

"Aaaaand." She drew out the word. "I'm considering redoing the living room. And of course I'm always behind on my magazine subscriptions."

Clare snorted.

"I don't see why that's funny," Ruth said.

Two more weeks passed. She wasn't sure why she cared so much.

"I read a couple of them," Ruth said, on the phone again. "But you know, sweetheart, I don't think I need to keep reading. I already know what happened."

Section Three

WHEN YOU CROSS THE SEA YOU LEAVE
WORRIES BEHIND

THE SHIP'S COOKS KNOW THAT SEA AIR GIVES
ONE AN APPETITE AND ACCORDINGLY PROVIDE
MOST EXCELLENT FARE.

She spends the first day lurching, swaying, holding on for dear life. Every step she takes is a pull to the water, a battle against her own solid, landlocked will.

She glances in the mirror in their little cabin, late in the morning of their first day at sea, and sees a reflection of her face so startling it almost quells the nausea, if only for a second: her skin is green, a pallor she has never seen before, as if she has been drained of color, and this vile, bloodless shade of sick is what rose up in its absence. Her lips, normally lush as a petal (she's vain about them, never needs lipstick), are gray.

(Long before Walter, before Max, Annelise would sometimes gaze at her own lips in the bathroom mirror and practice kissing herself. She was twelve, maybe thirteen, and she and Emmi and Sofie had just seen *The Chronicles of the Gray House* at the cinema. The enormous faces of the forbidden lovers coming together in the dark like pale moons had sparked something in her—something more than plain curiosity. She suspected that this would someday be a crucial skill, but there was no one to teach her. She took to standing a foot away from the little round bathroom mirror and moving slowly closer and closer, scrutinizing her mouth. "I love you," she would whisper to herself, fogging the mirror. "I must have you." Klara walked in once as Annelise was smashing her face against the glass: opened the door, saw the striking tableau of her daughter pressed against her own reflection, and clicked the door shut with such instinctive gentleness that Annelise, distracted by her affections, never even knew.)

On that first day in the middle of the ocean, Annelise throws up five times and wishes, finally and sincerely, to die. She swallows a Mothersill's Seasick pill, and prays.

Walter, naturally, is steady as a rock. If there is an opposite condition to seasickness, that's what he has: sea-heartiness, sea-wellness. He perches next to Annelise on the narrow bottom bunk in their neat, cramped cabin, Ruthie on his lap, and rubs his wife's back. She fixes her eyes on the wardrobe on the opposite side of the tiny room; if she extends her arm straight out in front of her, she could touch it. Its door is unlatched and swings open, clicks against the closet in time to the rolling waves. She holds on to a bucket so tightly her knuckles are white.

"Maybe if you come outside with Ruthie and me and get some fresh air you'll feel a bit better," Walter suggests.

He has no idea. Stand up? Come outside? She shakes her head, opens her mouth to tell him that she can't. Then the ship lists, and she thrusts her head into the bucket.

How lucky she is to have a husband who takes such good

care of her. Her friend Emmi, who immigrated to Australia, is married to a brilliant man—a promising and ambitious mathematician who worked at the university until they fired him—who insists on a rigorous daily schedule of meals and an unwavering standard of cleanliness. Even when Emmi was pregnant with their little Ellen and sick every day, he maintained his rigid expectations. Emmi told Annelise that some mornings she would scrub the toilet, vomit, scrub it again; what kept her going, she confessed, was her recurring fantasy of poisoning him.

How could you know the heart of your beloved before you married him? Courtship was a confection. Crisis brought out the best in people, or the very worst. But daily life, with its accidental farts and blood on the sheets, armpits and burned roasts, exposed you to the truth: an inflexible heart or an expansive one, contempt or compassion. How lucky Annelise is to have found such a caring soul in Walter. Tears slip down her face. She imagines (just for a second!) shoving her dear husband over the railing and into the sea. She wants her mother.

Walter stands, careful not to hit his head on the low cabin ceiling, hoists Ruthie into his arms. "Hi, Mama!" the baby says, as if just noticing Annelise for the first time. "Mama! Hi!"

"Hi, my sweetheart," Annelise manages. Ruthie reaches for her, and she reaches back, although she can barely hold her arms up. Even now, in her reduced state, there is this force between them. She feels it, sometimes, as hunger.

In the train station, dry-eyed, she watched her mother with Ruthie and forced herself to take note of every detail:

the two of them, heads together, a still image surrounded by chaos. Her mother, on her knees, clutching Ruthie. Her face an implosion of pain.

This was Annelise's doing. She was the cold instrument between them, the scissors, the knife. This impossible rending. She was the child and the mother. How could she be both? She leaned against her tan leather suitcase, felt the rush of people hurrying past her, heard herself inhale. They had to leave. But did they? There was always a choice! She was choosing her child. She made herself watch them until the bitter end of it, *the worst moment of my life,* she knew then, and it would always be true; she watched without flinching, the pulse in her neck pounding, forcing herself to face it. Ruthie's dimpled little hands patting Klara's back, comforting her grandmother, the sweetness almost unbearable. She watched until her husband pried Ruthie from her mother's arms, and her father lifted her mother from her awkward crouch and led her away.

"We'll leave you now," Walter says, and Annelise feels a snap of fear, but of course he just means that they're going up to the deck, and so she nods, smiles weakly, grateful.

She lies down on the smooth bed, sleeps for a bit, wakes disoriented, and sits up slowly.

They're traveling in tourist class. Their cabin is small, but the amenities are fine: the men's smoking lounge and the ladies' parlor, after-dinner dancing on deck, lavish meals (oh, God), organized games for the children, and nightly promenades, the moonlight (she imagines) illuminating the shim-

mering silks and iridescent taffetas of the glamorous ladies
of first class. There are moments when Annelise lets herself
pretend that this is a grand adventure.

Her mother took her shopping a week before their depar-
ture. Annelise stood in front of the mirror in a pale rose tea
dress with cap sleeves. She could have been anyone, getting
ready for anything.

The stores were still happy to take their money. ("Imagine
that," her father had said more than once over the past few
years. "Our money is just as good as theirs.") The salesclerk,
silent and efficient, wrapped the dress carefully in paper, and
Klara squeezed Annelise's arm so hard it left a red mark. That
same day her mother also insisted on buying her a dove-gray
traveling coat, though it was May, but you never knew—
probably the winters there were longer, the springs colder,
and so, Klara insisted, Annelise would need it. Klara also
bought her, to go with the dress, a wool slouch hat with a
grosgrain bow. "Too much, Mama," Annelise said, shaking her
head, putting a hand up to her undeserving hair. It was an
extravagance. When would she wear it? But Klara insisted,
her eyes watery, desperate, and so Annelise accepted her
mother's kindness with her own.

She imagines taking the hat out of its box now, placing it
on top of her frizzled hair, the light pink of the hat setting off
the green of her skin. She almost laughs at the thought of it,
which makes her suspect that she might be feeling a bit better. She takes a few deep breaths, straightens her stockings.
Up, she orders herself. She eases herself off the bed, stands.
Wobbles a little. Her stomach jumps, traitorous, but then
settles. *Walk to the door,* she thinks. *Down the hallway.* With

increasing vigor, she ventures out and up, toward the third-class deck, in search of Walter and Ruthie.

Even now, a day away from the wrenching good-byes, Annelise's mind gropes toward the future. She can't help herself. She feels the first inkling of what it might be like to live calmly. She can hardly remember how it was to look a neighbor in the eye and expect a smile in return, to stroll to the park—they were not permitted to take Ruthie to the park—and sit on a bench. To walk down the street without fear of a mob. It was—she can see this now, even one day away from it—the theft of her soul.

Letters from Walter's cousin in Milwaukee described snow, staggering amounts of it, and so that was what she pictured, even though it was May—a soft white landscape, quiet, safe. That was as far as her imagination took her.

She makes it up to the deck, where the roll of the ship is more gentle, and the scene there resembles, in fact, a park: women lounging under blankets on long wooden deck chairs, men talking, clustered in groups of three or four, small children playing games with balls tethered to poles, a few older girls skipping rope. The day is sunny and crisp and the sky is vast. Seagulls soar and screech overhead, their white wings flapping like bridal veils in the wind.

She scans the crowd for her husband and daughter, and for Oskar, who booked passage with them. Everyone looks vaguely familiar in the absence of a recognizable context: all forced, by the blank geography of motion, to focus on their leisure. They appear somewhat grim in pursuit of it.

She finds her way over to the railing and holds on to it with both hands, blinking down at the waves. The sea looks swollen, almost sentient. Her nausea has dissipated, a bad dream, and its absence is a lightness. She hasn't spotted Walter and Ruthie or Oskar yet, and so, for a moment, she is alone.

Their lives were dismantled. The thought of everything she left behind undoes her. So she will be content right here, on this ship, a day away from her parents and close enough to imagine that they have tickets on the next liner.

She turns her head just as a small girl in a ruffled white dress shoots past her, faster than seems possible on such short legs, chubby little *Würste*. A split second behind, just out of reach, the girl's mother chases her. The little girl squeals, delirious with joy, but Annelise catches a glimpse of terror in the mother's eyes. A small child is a weapon against itself. Annelise would have reached out and grabbed her if her reflexes were quicker.

"Stop now, Gerda, darling!" the mother calls out in a forced, singsong voice that Annelise recognizes as the official language of motherhood. "Let Mama catch you!" But Gerda is zigzagging across the deck, careening past the other passengers like a squirrel being chased. Annelise gasps, frozen. This child is going to catapult herself off the ship and into the sea. *"Gerda!"* her mother calls out again, and the little girl throws her arms up and swerves, still laughing hysterically, and heads straight for the railing. Annelise slaps her hand to her mouth and stifles a scream.

There was a moment, very early on. There were countless indignities, and she bore them all, because of course she did, this was everything she knew, this was her *life:* the boycott of the bakery, the endless decrees that popped up like weevils in flour—you could no longer go to restaurants, to swimming pools, to the park, to the movies. They expelled the children from the schools. Removed the college students from their degree programs. Each new regulation was a violence against them, but each on its own was—strangely—bearable.

She and Ruthie were walking home from the market on a clear autumn afternoon. Annelise was carrying a small bag of apples, thinking about making applesauce. The day was chilly and the sky was edging toward lavender. Ruthie was in her push stroller, wearing a hat and mittens and wrapped up in a cozy wool blanket so that only her eyes and nose were visible. A pretty woman and her four children were walking toward them on the sidewalk, the children in line behind their mother. They looked vaguely familiar to Annelise, but her mind was elsewhere. Her foolish mind was on applesauce.

Annelise nodded hello.

"Filth," the woman snarled. The viscous pearl of saliva landed on her coat before she knew where it had come from.

Revulsion, an instinctive recoiling. And, *How did she know?* And, doesn't matter how. And, *Oh, of course, the bakery,* like chatting with someone in line at a shop and saying, "Now, remind me how I know you?" and Ruthie, and revulsion, and pick up your stride, don't react, and what else? *What is this?* Humiliation. A juddering rearrangement of her bones.

She made it home, through the door, into the apartment. Took off her coat, hung it carefully on the hook. Unwrapped Ruthie from her layers. Touched the baby's hands, her feet, her soft, sighing body—protection from harm.

She set Ruthie on the kitchen floor with a pot and a wooden

spoon. Scrubbed the dried spit with a rag until her coat was spotless, until there was no evidence that it had even happened. To the background beat of Ruthie's sturdy drumming, Annelise debated whether she would tell anyone and decided not to. In the rough act of scrubbing, she knew.

It took everything she had not to believe the insult.

She would wear the coat again, because one didn't just discard a coat and go out and buy a new one. And later that night, she would peel and core and slice the apples, set them in the pot in a little bit of water and sprinkle them with cinnamon and the last of the sugar. Stir. Watch as they slowly softened, surrendered their flesh to the simmering liquid, turned a perfect pink, and began to bubble.

But this was not what she had wanted to do with those apples. What she had wanted to do with the apples was to shove them in a dark corner of the kitchen pantry in their paper bag. To pretend to forget about them. To leave them there, untouched, and let them rot.

Little Gerda, bolting across the third-class deck, a dervish. Her mother, calling, *Gerdaaaaaa*. Annelise, jogging toward them.

Twenty, thirty feet ahead, the child thuds into a man's legs, and he bends and scoops her up, laughing. *Where did you come from, little thing?* And then Gerda's mother catches up with them, and she's laughing, too.

And Annelise forces herself to slow down, catch her breath. There was never cause to worry. Was there? She straightens her back, walks past the three of them, the man already resuming conversation with his companions, hardly missing a beat, Gerda giggling in her mother's arms. She catches the woman's eye, searches quickly for a remnant of fear. There is nothing.

A few minutes later, Annelise, hand to her brow to block the sun, spots them. Walter is smoking a cigarette and talking to Oskar—she can see only his back. Then he turns and catches her eye, and she bites back a smile. They saw each other, of course, just the previous day, at port in Hamburg. Even so, a tiny jolt of electricity zaps through her, a little catch of happiness.

"Annelise," Walter says as she approaches. "I found him!" She reaches for Oskar's hand, and he grasps hers. Their mutual affection eclipses everything else for a second.

Walter pulls Annelise close and settles his arm around her waist, and the memory of that night flashes brightly in her brain. She can't recall the meal she had made that evening, but she remembers the mohnkuchen. She remembers the way Walter set his cigarette in the green ashtray, the end of the cigarette glowing red, smoke rising from it. She remembers the dress she was wearing: pale, silvery blue silk with white embroidered flowers along the neckline, tied in the back. Funny, she thinks now, standing on the deck of the ship, squinting at Oskar's sharp face backlit by the blinding sun; funny, the details that fade, the ones that linger.

Dear Lise, why have you asked Walter to give up smoking?

There are so few pleasures left! He needn't give it up entirely.

Why not encourage him to indulge with measure, as he was

used to it here?

The wind whips up, and Annelise tastes salt as her hair blows across her mouth. She sways just a little, leans into Walter and glances out at the ocean. The ship's speed is comprehensible to her only when she finds a still point in the water. She fixes her eyes now on a gull bobbing on a wave as the ship shoots ahead.

"So, with any luck Julius's and Klara's visas will arrive this week," Oskar says to her—a continuation of the same conversation they'd been having for months. "My sister's and mother's, I think, are still some weeks away." They might be in their kitchen, or sitting around the dining room table. Annelise feels the drumming of her heart in her chest. Next to them, a young woman reclines in a deck chair, a fashion magazine—*Modenschau*—hiding her face, her white calves bare.

"Well," Walter says, since Annelise hasn't replied, "at the very least, we'll be able to arrange the affidavits from America."

Oskar nods. He adjusts the small box he is holding—a camera—and worries it from one hand to the other. His angular face is so handsome, Annelise thinks, and then swallows a laugh. The shock of her own frivolous disloyalty! She rests her head on Walter's shoulder.

They talk for a few minutes in the hushed tones they have all grown accustomed to using over the past few years, the habit of furtive whispering that will never fully go away—will make them seem, years later, as if they are always anxiously planning someone's surprise party. Walter and Oskar tick off their list of mutual friends and acquaintances, nodding their heads: this one in Cuba, these three on their way to Shanghai. This one in Belgium, in England, Australia, Holland, New York. Safe, not safe, not safe, not yet.

But they're safe. Worry makes you vigilant, and fear makes you smart. What will it feel like when the cause for fear has passed? Annelise can't begin to imagine.

She looks around at the bustle, the oddness of movement on a moving ship. She can almost see the outlines of the shimmering ghosts of their old life. She feels a clench low in her belly even before her brain articulates her unease. She grabs Walter's sleeve in panic, hisses, "Where is . . ."

But Walter knows—of course he knows. He points to a small group of children just a few feet away, partially obscured by the sunbathing woman in the deck chair. Annelise twists a little and can clearly see. A little girl, nine or ten, has her arm slung protectively around Ruthie's shoulders, sweetly maternal. They're playing with dolls.

Relief shoots through her, hot shame on its heels. How many minutes had they been clustered here together, talking about other people, before Annelise even thought about Ruthie?

"How could you lose sight of her?" she demands, her voice high, even as she knows he hadn't.

Walter looks as though she has slapped him. "Lise," he says. "I would never."

"Would you allow me to take a photograph of your lovely family?" Oskar interrupts, a little dreamily, as if he knows he is wading into a dangerous swamp, or, on the other hand, has missed the last few moments completely.

"Yes, of course," Walter says. Annelise lurches away from her husband and goes over to grab Ruthie. The older girl's head is bent toward Ruthie. The ordinary contrast of her daughter's dark curls and the girl's blond pigtails calms her.

Annelise kneels down next to them, smoothing her brown skirt across her thighs. Ruthie meets her mother's gaze and then turns back to the dolls. The older girl doesn't want to be interrupted, either. She fixes Annelise with her very blue eyes and a grave little nod, and then arranges herself so that Ruthie is nestled between her outstretched legs.

"Hello," Annelise says. "What's your name?"

The girl waits a beat. "The mama dolly is taking the little girl dolly on a boat journey, right?" she whispers to Ruthie, then looks up at Annelise. "Eva."

"Eva, Ruthie is going to have her photograph taken now, but I'll bring her back in just a few minutes. Thank you for taking such good care of her."

Eva stares at her, a blank slate. "Do you promise I can have her back?"

"Of course."

The second Annelise scoops her up, Ruthie, wrenched from her playmate, bursts into tears. She screams and jams her fist into her mouth. She is furious, inconsolable. Her wails are like automobile horns blaring directly into Annelise's ears. "Ruthie!" Annelise says. "Stop it!"

Ruthie is such a good child. And so Annelise has fancied herself an excellent mother. But this is the third angry fit the little girl has had in as many days, and Annelise has no idea how to calm her. She is practically as flustered as Ruthie is. She remembers, long ago, Sofie telling her about Inge's tempers; it seemed, then, as if her friend were describing another country. Has her mother warned her about these frenzies? Has she counseled her on what to do? She can't remember. She needs to hear Klara's voice. Ruthie's shrieks drown out even her thoughts.

"No, Mama!" Ruthie screams, and she grabs a hank of Annelise's hair and pulls hard.

Before she can react, both men swoop in. Walter pries Ruthie, stiff and yowling, from Annelise's arms. Oskar, with the smile of the childless creeping up his face, cups his hand around Annelise's elbow to guide her. "Come," he says, ignoring the commotion. "Let's find a good place for this photograph," and leads them to a relatively empty spot on the deck, near the railing. "Give me a moment to focus the camera," he says, rotating the lens.

Standing, now, between her parents, arms raised and one hand clutched in each of theirs, Ruthie sobs. Annelise's scalp still stings in the spot where Ruthie yanked. She grips her daughter's hand, a little bit too tightly. She knows she owes her husband an apology, but, for now, she can't soften. Tension sizzles between them, crackles of electricity. Small patches of dampness spread under her arms; a tiny rivulet of sweat runs down her back. Ruthie wails on. "Child," Walter says quietly, under the din. "Enough."

Oskar adjusts his camera and whistles, undeterred. A sunbathing woman dozes peacefully nearby, the wind rustling the pages of her magazine. A blond girl drifts into and out of the corner of the frame, following the noise, searching for the small child she has befriended, has *loved*, whose mother has abruptly snatched her away without reason.

Behind them, the ocean sparkles.

This morning we received your letter and picture from New York. Why was that poor child crying so? I'm terribly homesick for my little girl.

For now we've decided not to sell the shop. What do you think about that?

Dear Walter, we have thought a lot about you lately because it's been quite hot here. How are you handling the heat there? And you, Annelise, and our sweet child?

I think that things don't look too good here.

At night, when the ocean is calm, the ship is a cradle. Annelise lies awake in their stuffy cabin, listening to her husband and daughter breathing, their snuffles and sighs a comfort, proof. She's suspended—between heartbreak and possibility, regret and relief. Soothed, despite the aching; eased, despite her fear. She is moving forward and backward at the same time.

At the train station, she squeezed her eyes shut and prayed that it was a dream. A quick reckoning: let her open her eyes and be ten years old, in her bed, waking from a nightmare. She would give up Walter and Ruthie for that. She would go that far back.

"You'll be safe," her father whispered to her. His rough cheek scraped against hers. "Do everything you can," he said. His voice was a plea, naked and bleak.

She can't sleep. The ship rocks, primal as a lullaby. Every heartbeat pulls her home.

Of course he is in love with her. And he has always been content to watch her. That's what he's doing now, on the ship: watching.

He has seen his share of beautiful women, many of them up close, in his office chair: sharp cheekbones, high foreheads, red bow lips, ice-blue eyes. Annelise is not that. But there is something about her face that moves him, something so dear and kind. Her face is beloved to him. Can that be? They know each other only in a certain way, as friends, connected through Walter. But she is beloved to him. She sees him. He sees her seeing him! So this, he thinks, is love: perfect vision. He is, after all, an optometrist.

He chuckles to himself, wishes he could share the joke with her. She's wrangling her little girl, kneeling next to the child, speaking quietly to her even as she is wailing. Oskar is watching.

There was that moment in the kitchen with her, washing dishes.

He can tell that her marriage makes her feel safe, protected, and that is what allows her to be open to him. He loves her in the space of that irony; right there is where he loves her, in that impossible space. And it has sufficed, and it will have to continue to suffice—this connection, this true thing shimmering between them.

Oskar lived with his mother and his sister in a small apartment. His father had died years ago, and his sister, Lucie, was a schoolteacher—although, of course, she had recently been fired. He lived with the women, his bedroom his only private space. He knew them with an intimacy usually reserved for young families, not a sixty-one-year-old mother and two grown children. He knew their coughs and their laughter and their flushes, the way the bathroom soap smelled slightly different on each of them. He ate dinner with them almost every night, and when he didn't, when he worked late or went out, they left food on the table, in a dish covered with an overturned metal bowl or a folded towel—meat, schnitzel or sausage, or a stew, potatoes, bread . . . he pretended that he lived an independent life, but he was taken care of by these women, and he, in turn, paid the rent, shared their expenses.

They sat down with him one Sunday evening and told him to go. They had saved, between them, enough money. Lucie had corresponded with a teacher in the States who had agreed to sign his affidavit.

They promised that they would manage until he could bring them over. He promised he would.

He can't stop looking at Annelise, the waves surrounding them, this woman, his friend's wife, rooted in this skimming moment. Over the past few months, she has become a more serious person, but they all are now. He can't take his eyes off her, her skin flushed, brown hair blowing in her face, her eyes on the camera but her whole body focused on her child—and Walter, his friend, right there at the helm of his little family. He sees only her. He waits as long as he can, and then he takes the photograph, and then he takes another.

On the fourth night of their crossing, when Ruthie is asleep, Walter and Annelise tiptoe out of their room and climb up to the deck. The wind is calm and the sky is thick with stars. She leans into Walter, and he wraps his arms around her waist.

Annelise is pragmatic. She understands the extent of her good fortune: it's as vast as the ocean. She and her husband and baby are moving toward safety. She will bring her parents to her. These thick knots will eventually loosen and fall away. Her choking fears will unclench in the soft bed she will lie in at night.

She will fill the jagged spaces—she has no choice—even though everything is breaking, and everything is lost.

*

Annelise woke up in her childhood bedroom on a Monday morning.

And five days later she lowers herself (her self still wobbly, having grown unaccustomed to solid ground) onto a chair in a yellow kitchen in a house just outside of New York City; and she stares at her husband, who has been made strange by the journey; and she holds Ruthie, who is delirious (teetering between ferocious sobbing and hysterical giggling, poor thing, poor little thing, be quiet, darling, *be quiet*).

After a few minutes of Mr. Maier asking anxious questions

about friends and relatives from home, Mrs. Maier, their kind hostess, notices that the little family is scraped hollow and cannot be expected to stay awake one second longer. She shushes her husband and lifts the baby from Annelise's arms, and Ruthie's head sinks like a stone onto the woman's unfamiliar shoulder.

And so on Saturday, Annelise lays her own head on a fat pillow on a bed in a strange house a world away from where she began.

Section Four

The train journey feels like a dream. The rhythmic motion lulls her brain into a kind of quiet. Walter sits across from her, looking out the window or paging through the same issue of the *New York Times* he's been painstakingly trying to read for a week. Every so often, he gets up and wanders into the smoking car and returns a few minutes later, and Annelise envies the habit of his that shapes the dull hours. Ruthie dozes next to her, her body heavy against Lise's arm.

Their compartment is airless, still. She has the feeling, removed from herself, in this enclosed space, listening to the repetitive clacking of the wheels against the tracks and gazing at the panorama of endless, greening prairie, that she might be able to stop time.

But instead the opposite happens: time folds them up and delivers them like a telegram. She is not ready! But now they're in Chicago, dusk falling. She holds her breath, exhales, heart thudding. More farmland, cows grazing and gentle green swells that look so much like the countryside around Feldenheim that she thinks, for a second, she might be losing her mind. And then Milwaukee, a city, their destination. How can your home be a name you can't even pronounce?

The driver can't (won't?) understand Walter's carefully practiced English, and Walter deflates a little, murmurs to Annelise, "You try." She manages.

And now they're here, at the front door of the large brick house on Newton Avenue. In the doorway, greeting them together, are Mr. and Mrs. Vogel.

"Ida and Alfred, please," Mrs. Vogel says. She takes Annelise's hand between hers and squeezes. Mrs. Vogel is so round that nothing defines the topography from her bust to her hips. "You are very welcome!" she says.

Mr. Vogel shakes Walter's hand, echoes his wife, "Welcome, come in!" His friendly little mustache bobs as he nods his head. The light behind the Vogels casts the living room in a warm glow, and Annelise aches with relief.

Ida Vogel is Walter's late mother's cousin, although Ida and her family left Germany when she was young, and the two women never met. Despite the distance, the Vogels agreed to sponsor Walter and Annelise, and so their common language is gratitude—given and received.

"Come, you must be famished. Dinner will be ready shortly. I had our housekeeper prepare a milk soup for the child." She extends her arm toward Ruthie and tries to shake the baby's hand.

Ruthie, irritable and exhausted and, Annelise thinks, a little feverish, pushes Mrs. Vogel's hand away, shakes her head *no*, burrows into her mother's shoulder and sneezes there.

"I'm so sorry," Annelise says, absorbing both Ruthie's sneeze and Mrs. Vogel's faint disapproval. "She's usually very friendly. It's been such a long week."

Ida Vogel is fifty-seven and barely remembers those end-less, ragged years when every woman she knew bloomed like a flower, and she spent her days lying on top of the bedcovers in her darkened room. She nods now at this pale, exhausted stranger and her beautiful, miserable baby, and ushers them all into the living room. "Maybe the child should go straight to bed."

Annelise swallows past a thick lump in her throat. Ruthie is exhausted, yes, but she needs to eat something before she'll sleep. "Yes, all right. Of course. I'll put Ruthie to bed."

They are family, but not family.

"No, Mama," Ruthie says, quietly at first, and then with increased hysteria. "No, Mama! No bed. No! No bed! No, no, no!" She is whipping her head back and forth, snot streaming down her nose.

Annelise, raw and disoriented, blinks hard. She looks around. Walter and Mr. Vogel have disappeared! A baby's cries, she has noticed, are a siren to men, a screaming alarm sounding the sudden, pressing need to be anywhere else. The two of them have probably scuttled down a long hallway into a smoking room somewhere in this cavernous house. Mr. Vogel has arranged a job for Walter in the shoe department of Gimbel's department store. They are probably smoking cigars and amiably discussing the latest trends in ladies' ankle straps while Ruthie howls.

"I think children are overindulged these days, don't you?" Mrs. Vogel says pleasantly, leading Annelise down the hallway to the guest room.

How old is she? Ida wonders. *Twenty-five? Twenty-six?* Walter's wife is young enough to be her own daughter, and yet Annelise—barely a woman, a girl—knows more about being a mother than she ever will. Ida clasps her hands together as she leads the way to the guest room, the room she and the housekeeper have spent days freshening with lovely new sheets, goose down pillows, laundered curtains, a vase of flowers. She presses the light on and glances at Annelise, hoping for a pleased reaction from the girl, but she is hushing her child, rubbing the baby's back, whispering to it, and so doesn't even notice the trouble Ida and the housekeeper have gone to for the newcomers. The immense trouble, frankly. With a little pinch of annoyance, she recalls those awful years—when all of her labors were small, irrelevant, ignored.

Earlier this afternoon she laid out an arrangement of decorative ornaments on a low table—a delicate crystal bowl, a blown-glass flower, and three little porcelain figurines. She sees now that this was a stupid mistake. Annelise is standing next to the table. The baby's pudgy legs are swinging inches above it, her feet fat little wrecking balls. How will she gather these fragile objects up without her guest seeing? She supposes she can't now, not without seeming rude: unacceptable conduct, rudeness—a fate worse than a few broken baubles. *Well, then,* she thinks. *Let them break.*

"We've put out fresh towels," Ida says. "Please take all the time you need. We'll wait dinner for you." She will always be deferential to the mothers. It's second nature to her now. No matter how young they are, how green, Ida knows her place: second-class citizen in the country of women.

Annelise nods and turns abruptly away from her hostess, and Ida backs toward the doorway and then into the hallway, softly clicking the bedroom door behind her.

*

Annelise squeezes her eyes shut for a moment as Mrs. Vogel closes the door. Ruthie sniffles, then wraps one moist hand around the starfish brooch pinned to Annelise's dress, slides the other into her hair.

"All right," Annelise murmurs, to Ruthie and herself. She gently pries the baby's hands loose and tries to lay her down on the bed. As soon as she does, Ruthie scrunches up her face and takes a deep breath, gathering her forces for a scream. Annelise snatches her up just in time. "It's all right," she says again. "Shhh."

All she wants to do is use the bathroom. Her desire to wash her face is practically carnal. She imagines the simple act of placing the baby in Klara's familiar, welcoming arms. The image is as vivid and real as the blank, bewildering moment she is actually in. Annelise counts backward to the last morning they were all together—a new habit that will stay with her. She inhales, a loud, staccato gulp of air.

Startled by Annelise's odd wheeze, Ruthie gives Annelise a quizzical look. Her brow furrows comically. The child's face registers everything she is thinking and feeling, and Annelise is a scholar of her expressions. She lowers herself onto the bed; the solid weight of Ruthie in her arms makes her knees crack. She has the feeling that their borders are dissolving, that her hand on Ruthie's back is Ruthie's hand, too; the baby's taut little body is an extension of her own arms. "It's just us," she whispers to her. Ruthie is no longer crying, but her eyes are glassy, and a thin, clear stream is now running from her nose. Annelise presses her lips to the baby's forehead and estimates a low fever, not frightening, but not negligible, either.

Take all the time you need, she thinks. *We'll wait dinner for you.*

She imagines herself emerging from this cloying, fussy guest room in a week, filthy and staggering. "Where is dinner? You said you'd wait dinner!"

She cups her hand over Ruthie's head. "Will you sleep?" she whispers. For lack of a rocking chair, she sways slowly, side to side, on the bed, and is brought back, for just a second, to the pitch of the ship. Ruthie whimpers for a while, fights it, but eventually her eyelids flutter, then close, her eyeballs darting under her lids as if they're transmitting code. After a few long minutes Annelise lays her down on the bed, so gently, knowing that the slightest jostle might wake her. Ruthie's mouth is half open, her arms and legs heavy, weighed down, finally, with sleep. Annelise takes a silent appraisal of her child and, for the thousandth time that day, she is completely reassembled by love.

An hour, Annelise thinks, as she silently arranges a fortress of pillows around the small sleeping body, an hour before Ruthie wakes up starving and furious.

I presume that by now you have arrived and that your trip was fine. Lise, tell me everything. How did Ruthie behave?

She tiptoes out of the room, careful to give wide berth to the table of fragile knickknacks—a little museum of danger, Annelise thinks, a collection of artifacts before they become shards.

Memories have been hurtling toward her since she left home: images, flashes, full and vivid scenes from the past, which is barely the past, brought forth by the implosion of time. The saturated violet of the spring sky before a thunderstorm. Her mother, laughing at something her father said, her face softening as she gazes at him, and Annelise, nine years old, suddenly and loosely and *angrily* apprehending the murky truth that her parents are separate from her, with a private connection that transcends her. A flash of Sofie passing her a note in class, white paper folded into a tiny square: an excellent drawing of Mrs. Jäger, their geography teacher, a large, stern woman with thick ankles and fleshy feet, whom Sofie has expertly transformed into a pig.

They were cruel sometimes, brutal in pursuit of a shared giggle. Annelise has neither the interest nor the ability to transform her memories into pleasant, blurred reproductions. She will take the images that come to her and examine them for blemishes or beauty, sharp spikes or soft edges. No matter. She'll take them all.

Now, standing outside the guest room, antennae quivering for the sound of Ruthie's breathing, she catches her own breath before she makes her way through the house, and a moment careens into her, wild and punishing: she is in the bakery (of course), washing a baking sheet in the middle of the morning (dreamy, the way she was, lost in her thoughts) and her mother brushes past her—her mother, a whirling taskmistress, a tempest of efficiency. As she passes, Klara's elbow jabs into the soft part of Annelise's side, just below her ribs, and Annelise gasps in pain. Klara doesn't notice. She is already on the other side of the large kitchen. And would she have cared if she had noticed? No! The pointillist painting of Annelise's emotions comes into focus at that moment, takes on clarity and sharpness. *My mother is a monster!* she thinks. *I hate her!* The theatrics of the realization feel right and righteous and true. Annelise savors her fresh hostility slowly, as if it's a hard, sweet butterscotch candy. Only later does the guilt set in, turns the candy bitter and gritty, like she is sucking on dirt.

She'll take every memory, even this one, because each image is a continuation of who she was, a reunion with herself. She'll take even this one: the sharp thrust to the ribs, the syrup of hate, the regret.

If you would like to have the piano, then of course I won't sell it. Can you use the dining room table?

Tomorrow is my Ruthie's birthday. I wish I could hug and kiss her. But I'm going to buy her a little doll, since she threw her doll down the toilet.

They really are waiting for her at the table.

"I sold the store," Walter is saying, "to an employee. If we go back someday, he assures me . . ." Walter stops and looks down, unable to finish the sentence he's been repeating for months, maybe (Annelise thinks as she watches him from the edge of the room) finally aware of how deluded it sounds.

"Annelise!" Mrs. Vogel says, pushing her chair back from the table. "Come sit!" She pats the place between her and Walter and rushes off into the kitchen, comes back a minute later carrying four steaming bowls of soup on a tray.

They eat the first course in silence, focused on the chicken soup, salty and comforting. Annelise glances up: at the crystal vase and the bouquet of dried flowers on the sideboard, the silver candlesticks and the pretty little cut-glass salt and pepper shakers on the table, at the light blue walls, at the shiny round bald spot on the top of Mr. Vogel's head as he bends toward his bowl.

In the silence every careful spoonful of soup is as loud as a gallon of water being sucked down a drain, and it takes them days to finish, years, Annelise just about panicking trying to reach the bottom of her bottomless bowl. Spoons clink like a tuneless bell choir. When they are finally done, Alfred Vogel looks around with a mischievous smile and says, "Well, that was really something!" And Ida laughs and lightly slaps his arm, and the spell is broken.

They talk, then, about what it's like, because the Vogels want to know. "We read the newspapers, and of course we receive letters from Alfred's cousins, but we want you to tell us. Can you tell us?"

Walter reaches for Annelise's hand, and she feels the pulse of his thoughts for the first time since they left Germany, the telepathy of marriage that has been wavering for days.

"The people you saw every day," he says, "your neighbors, your customers. Shopkeepers. Police officers. People stopped coming into the store, and then they stopped looking you in the eye, and then they began to hate you. People you trusted. Their affection turned sour"—he snaps his fingers—"like *that*. How do you make sense of it? I can't."

Annelise feels a flush rising to her cheeks, a wave of anger as elemental as thirst. "It's not safe to walk in the streets," she says carefully. She lets go of Walter's hand and places hers in her lap, where she twists her napkin into a rope. "Do you understand? Our neighbor was arrested, and the school-teacher as well. Arrested and beaten." She feels this now, allows herself. Rage, now that they are finally safe. "My parents' business was taken from them. They think we're animals," she says, and it all zaps through her, lightning in her body, hot, frying bolts of fury. Her teeth are buzzing. Filthy animals. She shakes her head. There's no way she can explain what it has been. "We're the same people we always were." Annelise's voice rises. Same people they were two years ago, last week. "Just the same!"

"We became ghosts in our own lives," Walter says.

Mr. and Mrs. Vogel are looking at them both. Mrs. Vogel has pressed her lips together into a white line. Mr. Vogel's face has gone pale.

"My parents," Annelise says.

"You can't imagine," Walter says softly, and that is insufficient, but possibly the truest thing.

What do you do all day, when Walter is gone? Do you take a lot of strolls with Ruthie? Can you have conversations with her?

Nothing is going to come of the couch and the upholstered chairs that were ordered. All together we don't quite know yet what to bring along, even though that may still be a long time in the future.

Annelise follows Mrs. Vogel into the kitchen and helps her bring out the rest of the meal: a brisket; a challah, egg-shiny and golden; a big bowl of green beans covered in butter. Two bottles of good Riesling.

She's hungry, hungrier than she's been in weeks. She had worried about it, a little, before they left—what would American food be like? Would she be forced to eat things she'd never seen before—strange berries; giant, fibrous squashes; gamy prairie birds? Would the unfamiliarity leave her finicky and unsatisfied? But now, chewing, swallowing: it's a relief.

"We're doing what we can," Mr. Vogel says. It sounds like an apology. But what do they have to be sorry for? "I write letters to our officials, which go unanswered. Ida collects money for the Aid Society."

"And of course we are sponsoring you," Mrs. Vogel adds. "Our refugees."

Mr. Vogel is slicing the piece of meat on his plate into tiny morsels. Ida catches Annelise watching him. "Alfred grew up in a large family," she says.

"Eleven children!" He laughs. "You had to make your portions last." He pauses, looks around his fine table in his well-appointed home. "Because you didn't get a second helping."

Annelise glances down at her plate, her mound of beans, a thick hunk of challah, her own serving of meat already gone, only a tide pool of gravy remaining. Heat rises to her cheeks, the shame of her appetite. She sets her silverware down, blots her grease-slicked lips. Her hunger is gone, demolished. Walter, next to her, stabs another slice of brisket and dredges it through the gravy on his plate.

She is using the proper fork, remembering good posture. Pretending to be an adult. Biting the inside of her cheek to stop herself from wailing. "We're so grateful to you," Annelise says. "We'll never be able to repay you." Embarrassed, she takes a sip of water.

"My dears," Mr. Vogel says, "you don't—"

"—owe us anything!" Mrs. Vogel finishes.

"You owe us nothing," Mr. Vogel says again, his voice thick with emotion.

Annelise understands, then, that this is how Ida and Alfred Vogel love each other, with no children of their own to bind them.

The crash from the other room shocks them all, even the two who saw it coming: the high music of shattering glass, then shrieking. Annelise is the first up and out of her chair, quick as a shot through the dining room and the hallway. Mrs. Vogel, surprisingly nimble, is close at her heels. Walter and Mr. Vogel are probably right behind them, but Annelise doesn't see, doesn't care. *Oh, God,* someone is murmuring. *Oh, God.*

She is suspended in thick terror in the seconds it takes to reach the guest room door, frozen in the limbo of not knowing. Better to be immobilized in this moment than to push open the door and find blood, disaster. But you can never pause. You have to find out.

She feels the pressure of Walter's hand on her back, barrels through the door.

Ruthie is standing, gripping the edge of the table, tiny girl at a tiny table, screaming. Annelise rushes to her. Glass crunches beneath her feet. Ruthie's face is red, eyes closed, mouth open. Annelise knows immediately that these are not screams of pain, but she doesn't trust the knowing, and so she scoops her up and lays her down on the bed in one smooth motion, strips her, examines every inch for injury, for damage, for blood. Every inch of her: plump elbows, delicate skin between her fingers, the creases of her knees, her thighs, her seashell ears, the tendons in her neck. She scans the clean, white bedspread for errant drops of blood.

Walter is standing over them. Annelise turns to say something to him and flinches. His eyes are dark with worry. Fear has slackened his features. He has used up a measure of strength from a quantity that is not bottomless.

"She's not hurt," Annelise says.

He exhales. "I thought—"

"She's not."

Walter, because he is a salesman, a reader of faces, sees what is on his wife's: the flicker of disappointment. She looks up at him and thinks she sees fear, weakness.

But he is not afraid. Ruthie's screams cut him past the bone, down to the steel at his core. When he raced to his daughter, he was whispering a prayer: asking for nothing, promising vigilance.

*

Walter's hand on Annelise's back, her hands on Ruthie. She picks up the naked, sobbing child and is immediately drenched in the baby's warm urine.

The crystal bowl is shattered, the glass flower snapped at the stem. The three porcelain figurines are unharmed, futile guards against the siege. Annelise turns to Ida to apologize for the wreckage, but instead of remorse, hot lava rises in her, and she is silent.

Ida Vogel stares back, her expression inscrutable.

That night, the first night in their new city, she reaches for Walter. She takes his hand, maps out the bones of it with her fingertips as he blinks awake. She turns onto her side and moves close to him, into the dip in the middle of the bed, the length of her body against his, her thighs pressing into his thighs, stomach to stomach, chest to chest. He exhales, grins in the dark; he is a little taken aback, and game. He wraps his arms around her and kisses her forehead, murmurs something into her hair. Her own skin feels hot, her thoughts blurred. She may be fevered herself. The baby lies in a cot next to them, restless in sleep.

He props himself up on one elbow, leans over her, pulled by the same magnet. Desire is the stupid cousin of hope: blunt biology, ceaseless propagation. A flicker of light in the fathomless dark. Even in the heat of wanting, she can see that! But still. Body to body, alive and starving, she wants, and wants, and wants.

*

They are guests of the Vogels for four weeks, until their apartment becomes available. Annelise spends every day of those four weeks wound up and terrified of another disaster. Every time Ruthie touches something, she jumps up and takes it out of the baby's hands. Her right eye twitches. Her jaw aches. *I can't,* she whispers to Walter late one night in their dark room. *I cannot take another minute of this!* and then they both laugh, because *this,* of course, is nothing. Not a thing. Still, she's a wreck by the time the month is finally over.

The moment they walk in the door of their new home, she feels a little click of recognition as she steps back into her own skin.

And until the day she dies, Mrs. Vogel will recall with fondness the loud, messy month when her house was full.

What I gather from your letters, dear Annelise, is homesickness. We are as far apart from you as you are from us. Some days I just cannot bear the thought of being apart from you.

You keep reminding me that I should take care of myself. I do. If I just had more of an appetite. I'm always cold.

You write that I don't answer the questions you raise in your letters. Until now, I have answered each and every one! But you owe me some answers, my dear.

———

Fear comes for her, clutching at her chest, clawing at her thighs. She thinks, *No.* She thinks, *I'm safe, we're safe.* But the fear wings around her ears and licks its lips, chomps its teeth. *Never safe,* it whispers, laughing.

Walter leaves for the store early, six days a week. Annelise cleans houses and takes in laundry, jobs she can do with the baby in tow—a familiar use of her skills, and she doesn't let herself feel anything but gratitude. Days when she doesn't have paying work, she walks with Ruthie.

Back home, she was known for her terrible sense of direction. Sofie and Emmi loved to remind her of the time she got lost walking to school—a route she took every single day, just four blocks from home. But she was so distractible, more attentive to random details (her favorite blue cornflowers growing in a clump by the side of the street, a cat prowling in a bush) than to the precision of the outcome, the distance of long blocks, where to turn right, where to turn left.

Here, alone, with just the baby, she's careful. For weeks, she allows herself to walk only in a straight line, so that she can't possibly get lost, so that when she's ready to go home, she just has to turn around.

She's all right, for a while, taken in by the tranquillity of her new neighborhood, bamboozled by it: the children playing outside; the profusion of trees, their long boughs stretching overhead like arms reaching for one another; wide, clean sidewalks; the duplexes with their windows open to warm breezes. In one of the apartment houses on her block, someone plays piano every day at four; a few houses away, an aspiring opera singer practices scales. Annelise walks up and down the street with Ruthie and hears music.

After a few weeks, boredom sets in, and a little twitch of curiosity, so she decides to broaden her scope. Four blocks south, then one left turn. The main street is just three more blocks east. She knows, because Mrs. Vogel showed her: here, the meat market; across the street, the greengrocer. Over there, just at the end of the block, a tailor, and next to him, a bakery. "A bakery! You'll feel right at home!" Mrs. Vogel said, patting her arm. Annelise and Walter navigate these streets together on the weekends, but she's never done it alone.

After the left turn, the panic hits. The street is crowded with midday shoppers, mostly women. In their hats, their summer dresses, they could be the same women who bustled up and down the busy streets in Feldenheim, housewives with their minds on dinner, mothers, like her, lulling their babies to sleep with motion. Women in search of a good loaf of dark bread. And the men, wearing uniforms, working.

Where is she allowed? She catches herself looking for signs in windows telling her she can't go in. The glass shop windows here are blank, as blank as the faces of the women.

She grips the handles of the stroller. Her vision blurs, her throat constricts. She's jolted back to the fear of her other life, a familiarity so deep it's almost friendly. Where is she? For a second, she doesn't know.

Here, safe. She's in front of the greengrocer. She lifts the baby from the stroller, hoists her onto her hip, and walks into the store, realizes too late that she can't carry Ruthie and a bag of carrots and potatoes and onions at the same time. She's noticed that other women leave their children in their strollers in front of stores. She, of course, will never do that; she'd sooner go hungry.

"*May ei hel pyoo?*" a man in a white apron asks her. She can't understand him, not even a little bit; all she hears are syllables, a congealed collection of sounds. She shrinks into herself, feels tears rising. *Hel pyoo?* he repeats. *Fein sumpf resch froot?* Annelise shakes her head. The man shrugs, smiles—in another life, it would have been a reassuring smile, but in this one, Annelise sees pointy teeth, a lupine grimace. She hurries away, goes back outside, settles Ruthie into her seat. Two women walk past her, laughing. A crow swoops low and caws, settles onto a nearby tree branch. Cars clank by. The street is a confusion of menace. Home is three blocks west, four blocks north. A piano, a birdbath, an opera singer, a small garden of blue irises. Her hammering heart. The cold sweat on the back of her neck. Puffy clouds scuttling across the bluest sky. Will she have to do this again tomorrow? The next day? Walter will not complain when dinner tonight is bread and butter, yesterday's soup.

You keep writing that we should buy our tickets, but first

we will have to get our visas and other permits.

This is her street now. These are the wooden steps that lead up to her front door, the peeling paint on the railing. This is the way the key catches, then turns the lock. Annelise is the key. She is the moment: stuck tight before she loosens, then finally gives.

She knows of Charlotte, knows her habits, weeks before she meets her. Annelise cleans for the Fischers, on Kenwood Boulevard, and she knows that their niece is living with them, another refugee from Germany, a girl who has no other family. She's a dressmaker, this niece, and the Fischers have set up a studio for her on the ground floor of their house. Annelise sweeps the stray threads and snips of cloth from the workroom floor, runs a feather duster over the hard curves of the dressmaker's dummy (and feels a vague sense of perversion whenever she does), crumples up old newspaper and scrubs the full-length mirror with vinegar and water. But she has not met the seamstress herself.

After her first few times alone in the empty studio, Annelise names the dummy Hildegard and begins to have little chats with her while she cleans and straightens. "Excuse me, dear Hildegard, I'm so sorry for disturbing you," she murmurs as she wipes the wooden stool the dummy is perched on. "Hildegard, you're looking well," if she hasn't been to the Fischers' in a while.

"That's not her name!"

Annelise spins toward the voice in the doorway, her face hot. A young woman stands there, a girl, pale and tiny in a pretty green and white polka-dotted dress, and smiling. "It's not Hildegard." She moves toward Annelise, then veers over to the dummy. *"Hildegard!"* she says again, directly to the mannequin. "You're much more sophisticated than that, aren't you?" She turns to Annelise and nods once. "Dorothea."

Flustered, Annelise wipes her hand on her apron, then sticks it out to shake. "Dorothea," she says, "I'm Annelise."

The girl laughs. "No, no. Annelise, it's my pleasure to meet you. I'm Charlotte Fischer, and *this* little girl is Dorothea." She pats the dummy's hard shoulder. Charlotte's voice is a robin's high chirp. "She happens to be the only other girl I talk to some days. Until today."

Annelise feels the hot blush fading. When was the last time she spoke to another young woman her age? How many months? She points her chin toward the mannequin. "She's very good company. Hardly ever argues."

"Oh," Charlotte says, shaking her head sadly. "You don't spend as much time with her as I do. She can be very contrary. Doesn't like it when I come near her with my pincushion."

"Well, who can blame her?"

Charlotte pauses, pretends to consider. "Hmm, I never thought of it that way! I'm really sorry, Dorothea!"

Annelise is a girl again, and Charlotte is Sofie, is Emmi, and they are two girls delighted with each other.

———

Alone at the kitchen table, she writes to her mother.

How is Erna Silber (whose husband and son were arrested in November)? *How are the Weisses* (forced to sell their store for practically nothing)? *Mrs. Zimmermann* (whose husband took his own life two months ago)?
   The baby is chatting away now. Every day we show her the photograph of you both, and of course she remembers you.
   We're doing everything we can.

How is it that the Germans want them gone but make it nearly impossible to leave? The contradiction gnaws at her, incomprehensible: an intimate betrayal and a swirling bureaucracy of cruelty. There's nothing they can do but wait.

You'll be with us soon.

Every bright sentence casts a shadow of deception.

The next time Annelise sees Charlotte, she invites her over for lunch, then asks Walter to invite Oskar, too—a little gathering of friends in their new home.

Charlotte arrives a few minutes early with a dress she's made for Ruthie, gingham, ruffled at the hem, with a Peter Pan collar. "I can take it in if it's too big," she says. "I had to guess." She runs her palm over the fabric as if she's saying good-bye to a friend, and hands the dress to Annelise.

Ruthie is playing in the corner, kneeling in front of a little wooden dollhouse and talking softly to herself.

Annelise holds the dress, speechless. It's a perfect pink concoction, spun sugar. Annelise herself is wearing a plain navy wool skirt and a blouse she's had to mend twice, purchased nine years ago at a shop in Feldenheim. She guides Charlotte into the small living room, newly aware of the cracks in the ceiling, the stains on the old carpet, every secondhand plate on the table.

Charlotte watches Walter as he hangs her coat in the closet; she stares at Ruthie in the corner, then reaches for Lise's elbow, almost as if to steady herself.

Oskar arrives. The late-morning light tips through the windows, and the scent of the apple cake that Annelise has baked fills the little apartment. It's the first sweet thing she has made since they arrived here. It's her first concession to pleasure.

I think that I might get my visa sometime this week at Mainz.

Hopefully we'll have more luck now.

If you can, put in an extra affidavit for your father.

I would have written sooner, but I was ill again. But I'm feeling better now, and I can manage things. I'm sure if I were with you and my sweet Ruthie, I would quickly recover. If only my nerves would be a little stronger.

In a kitchen that will never quite cooperate with her instincts, in an apartment so small that it sometimes feels like it is actually shrinking, Annelise rubs a raw chicken gently with salt and pepper. She carefully eases a lemon and a few cloves of garlic into its cavity. The preparation is an intimate, fleshly task, and it feels to her at times like a violation.

Walter is still at work. Ruthie is asleep, probably for another ten minutes. So for the moment on this darkening Friday afternoon it's just the two of them in the kitchen, Annelise and this particular chicken. She stops her work for a second and regards it: splayed, goosebumped, headless.

Annelise trusses the poor chicken, wrapping twine around the bones of its scrawny back legs. She will never get used to the light in this kitchen, the way it falls through the low window in the morning, dimming throughout the day just as she needs more brightness, not less. It's as if the person who built this kitchen didn't understand labor, or time. She pours a bit of oil into her cupped palm and drizzles it over the body of the chicken.

So much of this new life is her hands. Pointing to items in stores when she can't remember the word. (And she gets so nervous, she often can't remember the simplest words. Bread! It's practically the same in German! She is a fool in this language.) Digging around in her handbag for her keys: one for the main door, another for the door to their apartment, always confusing the two. Massaging Walter's shoulders after a long day at the store. Gripping Ruthie's hand in busy, unfamiliar crosswalks. Measuring flour, chopping carrots, holding a pen, filling out paperwork over and over. Not to mention wringing out other people's clothes, sweeping other people's floors.

Once an animal, now food. She deposits the chicken into the oven and washes up, unties her apron, begins to set the table. Their beautiful dishes did not survive the journey— almost all of them chipped or cracked in transit. The dishes they have now are white with a garish pink-cabbage-rose border, given to them by the refugee committee. She hates them.

Has she been imagining Oskar's attentions? The lingering glances, the way he touches her arm when he's making a point—is her mind playing tricks on her, an echo of that moment, years ago, when she conjured the trace of his fingers down her spine?

Oskar always comes with little gifts—once an orange glass elephant, once a pencil sketch he drew of a poodle standing on its hind legs. Last week he brought a small box of sugary apple candies, two weeks ago a roll of Choward's violet mints, after she told him they were her favorites. Everyone else assumes these presents are for Ruthie, and Ruthie lays claim to them with glee (even the violet mints, which she spat out immediately, to the amusement of the adults). But Annelise knows: the presents are meant for her. And in that knowing, she lives a life in Oskar's thoughts. *What would she like,* she imagines him wondering. *What is she like?*

Lise and Walter are working every angle. The documents fly back and forth between Milwaukee and Washington, DC, like migrating geese. They're spending a small fortune on stamps alone. Visa applications, documentation, affidavits of support. Proof of financial endorsement. Proof of money. Proof of future money. Actual money.

> *I beg you most urgently, please try immediately to get the affidavit of support for us. Go through the special number for parents. . . .*
>
> *Yesterday we received the affidavit of support from Stuttgart, but unfortunately it wasn't right again. Everything is examined to the smallest detail. You have to have an additional guarantee, otherwise we will be turned back again. Please fill out things a little bit more carefully next time. Go through it point by point.*
>
> *I know that you are doing everything possible. We are not the only ones who have received their affidavits back several times. You have to examine everything very carefully.*

It gets harder, never easier. Annelise is bird-walking across a wire: unbelievable good fortune on one side, unfathomable heartbreak on the other. Sometimes, at night, after she puts Ruthie to bed, she is too tired to speak.

As she places the last glass on the dining room table, she hears sniffling from the bedroom, little whimpers. *"Mamaaaaa,"* Ruthie sobs, and Annelise hurries to her, low heels ticking across the floor.

"I'm right here," she says as she opens the door to Ruthie's darkened room, reassuring them both. "Everything is all right." Annelise bends toward her, eyes still adjusting. Ruthie takes a deep breath and wraps her arms around Annelise's neck. She carries Ruthie into the kitchen (although the little girl is perfectly able to walk), unwraps her, sets her at the table with paper and crayons, smooths a sleep-damp strand of hair from her forehead.

"I'm hungry," Ruthie says. "And I wet my pants."

Rest the chicken before carving, Klara taught her. Can you envy a dead bird? Just a little?

Oskar and Charlotte arrive right on time, bearing (as she knew they would) a store-bought chocolate cake larded with icing. Charlotte is a busy working woman; her dressmaking business is thriving. "Thank heavens for good bakeries!" she says every time. Oskar cradles the white pastry box, and Charlotte holds lightly to his arm.

Walter ushers them inside, happy to see them: *Hello, welcome, my friends, welcome,* as if they have not been walking into this apartment for dinner every single Friday night for the past two years. He shakes Oskar's hand, then Charlotte's, then Oskar's again. Annelise, a step behind, marvels at her husband. He is always so ready to be pleased—to sift pleasure from worry, in spite of everything.

Ruthie charges into the living room, flying elbows and thumping feet, and flings herself at Oskar, who slides the cake over to Walter just in time and scoops her up, swings her around.

"Hi!" she yells. "Hi, Uncle Oskar! Hi, Aunt Lotte!" She swivels her head, makes sure she has everyone's attention. "I have been drawing some pictures, and Mama gave me an apple!" At four, she is more at ease in English than the adults will ever be. "I certainly don't expect a present!" she adds, as Oskar sets her down. Annelise explained to her last week that it was impolite to demand gifts.

"You don't?" Oskar says, crouching to meet her. "That's too bad. Then what will I do with this?" He looks at Annelise and smiles, pulls a small toy out of his jacket pocket—a wind-up frog. Oskar demonstrates, turns the key and the little green and yellow tin frog hops high into the air. Ruthie squeals.

There is—maybe, just—an understanding between the two of them, a fleeting feeling of another life, a shared ache. It has nothing to do with Walter or Charlotte. Annelise is certain of that.

She takes Oskar's suit jacket, Charlotte's lemon-yellow spring coat (too thin for this weather!), hangs them in the closet. "Dinner is almost ready."

Charlotte squeezes Annelise's arm and follows her, back into the kitchen and away from the men. "I have to tell you something," she whispers, with a giddy little laugh.

Annelise shuts the kitchen door for privacy. The heat from the oven fills the room. She faces Lotte, takes her in: tiny, compact, brown hair curled and swept up in front, eyes bright, Arpège perfume a faint, sweet floral cloud around her. "What is it?"

"Lise, you know the wedding dress I'm sewing for Jennie Weil?" Her hands swiftly describe its shape, nipped waist, full skirt. Annelise nods. Charlotte is in the process of sewing the wedding dress for the middle daughter of one of the wealthiest Jewish families in Milwaukee. The wedding will take place in early September.

"Well!" she says, stepping closer. "Mrs. Weil stopped in yesterday." She giggles and claps her hand to her mouth for a second. "Oh, promise you won't tell anyone! I just can't keep it a secret!"

Annelise is swept into the story. Charlotte has a knack for capturing a person's attention. "I promise! What is it?"

"They've asked me to let out the dress." She holds her hands up next to each other, then widens the space between them. "And to finish it quickly." She leans in so close, Annelise can see the faint orangish line on her chin where her makeup didn't quite blend into her skin. "They're moving the wedding date up to *June!*"

Annelise pauses, tilts her head. "Hmmm. I don't understand. Why the fuss? So she's gained a bit of weight, so they want to marry in spring instead of fall?"

"Lise!" Charlotte says, eyes bright and surprised. "But don't you . . . ?" and then Annelise laughs, and they're both laughing, and Annelise embraces her friend. She loves her for this: for bringing her silly gossip on a Friday evening, a gift, as if this is all they will ever need to care about.

"So," Lise says, "they'll have a rather large baby born seven months after the wedding. *Mazel.*"

Low laughter rolls in from the living room, exactly as it used to, only now with the accompaniment of the high, sweet flute of Ruthie's voice. Annelise remembers the table that she didn't finish setting earlier, the bread cooling on the wire rack, the chicken still in the oven. Remembers Oskar, remembers her husband. Remembers, in a sudden stab, the duality that she carries with her every second, without respite: here and there; this life, that life. She swallows her own guilt along with a sharp, surprising lump of resentment for Charlotte. But it's not Lotte's fault for bringing gossip! It's the fault of the world, for containing it.

Charlotte, still giggling, turns and bangs into the slightly open silverware drawer. "Oops!" she says, rubbing her hip. "Lise, please, let me help you with dinner."

After a pause, Annelise says, "It would be a huge help to me if you would play with Ruthie." Charlotte is so good with her, always has been. "The men are probably just popping candy into her mouth. But she really needs to be distracted. She's been underfoot all day." With a hand on her friend's shoulder, Lise guides Charlotte back into the living room, where Ruthie is, indeed, running amok, twirling between the chair and the sofa. Annelise pulls a few toys out from the bureau, a stuffed bear, a ball, a Raggedy Ann doll.

Her heart settles, like a liquid into the contours of its container.

Walter, from his perch on the sagging sofa, arms crossed over his chest, surveys his kingdom, this tiny second-floor apartment: brown carpeting in the living room, threadbare in places; buckling linoleum in the kitchen; rattling windows; furniture showing signs of wear. Ruthie's bedroom is small, and their own is minuscule, practically a closet. In the dining room, narrow as a hallway, there is space for their table and nothing else. Lise keeps the apartment spotless and bright, but it's nothing like their home in Feldenheim, and it never will be.

Oskar sits in the armchair across from the sofa. Ruthie and Charlotte are crouched in the corner, chatting. The hem of Charlotte's skirt has ridden up her thigh, exposing the top of her stocking, the pale clip of her garter. Walter looks, then looks away.

There is an ocean of difference between what you give up and what is stolen from you. Lise cleans houses and takes in laundry so that they can make ends meet, and she never complains, but sometimes, at the end of the day, in the dark, shocking quiet, he sees that there are parts of her that are closed to him now, inaccessible. And he sees—tired as he is, he sees—the looks his wife and his best friend exchange, the little spark that flickers between them. He has already decided to let it be. He knows not to feed oxygen to a fire.

She imagines Oskar's mouth on hers, her hands on his face— the fantasy is so vivid and awful, she almost drops the pitcher of water she is carrying. She imagines his body against hers (and sets the pitcher down, there), pressing against her in the cramped kitchen, his hands on her shoulders, her waist, urgent—or, no, maybe not urgent, maybe gentle and light, easy.

The daydream swallows her; she expands inside of it. She misses her mother's bossy demands, the little chirp she would make when she slipped off her shoes as she walked in the door; how, every day of Annelise's childhood until the day she moved out, Klara fluffed up her bed pillows—a tiny, indisputable admission of her very disciplined love.

Annelise removes the challah from the oven now, sets it on the wire cooling rack.

Oskar reminds her of Max, if she's honest with herself: a little bit difficult, unpredictable. She wants to tell him everything and not feel the sting of betrayal.

She pulls a kitchen chair over to the pantry, climbs up, pulls the brass candlesticks from the top shelf: one in each hand, her balance precarious. The sounds from the living room reach her; she is at once present and absent from this moment, a hallway away from everyone she loves on this continent. She eases herself down and off the chair, still holding the candlesticks—like trophies, like torches.

She wonders when Charlotte will become pregnant. How will she tolerate it? It's been four years, but Annelise recalls it all: not just the physical upheaval and discomfort, but also the growing knowledge that you are not yourself, not solely—no longer contained within the delicate capsule of your own skin. And then the baby, crashing into your life like some being from another world, your fault and your terrible responsibility. What kind of woman will Charlotte be then, Annelise wonders of her friend, what kind of mother? Will her children be slightly unkempt, the kind for whom other mothers pack an extra lunch? Or will Charlotte rise to the occasion, fully dedicated, focused and calm?

"We have to take care of her," Walter said to Annelise, just the other night, after Lise gingerly suggested they take a Friday night to themselves. "She needs us," he insisted. "She's alone."

"She's not alone! She has Oskar! We're just as alone as she is!" They were lying in bed together, on their backs, side by side. Her face was damp with skin cream. Walter smelled, as always and not unpleasantly, of soap and leather. He hooked his leg lightly over hers.

"We're not in competition for who is most alone. You know Oskar can be impatient with her. So, Lise, why not make a meal for them? We have enough to share."

Walter is so generous. She's lucky, in that way.

Her mother's letters to her are urgent and pleading, even angry. Every minute that passes without approval for their visas feels more desperate and impossible, and in the midst of it all, Annelise finds, she can somehow still feel these petty things: jealousy, irritation, the odious, intolerable sense of being both fortunate (to be here, to be safe) and overburdened at the same time.

In the kitchen, she rests her elbows on the countertop, just for a moment, cups her face in her hands and closes her eyes.

Oskar wanders in with his wineglass. "My dear," he says.

They are so gentle with each other, the most beautiful accessory of their European manners.

She straightens, pats her hair down. Heat rises to her face. "Endless worries," she says.

He nods, opens the cupboard, and takes a glass down as if he lives here. He pours a glass of wine and passes it to her, and although she doesn't like wine, she sips. It's sweet and cold as it slips down her throat.

*

Charlotte and Ruthie are laughing together on the living room floor. Annelise walks over to them, crouches down to see what they're doing, gently slides Charlotte's hem back down her leg. Charlotte doesn't even notice. But Walter, out of the corner of his eye, sees his wife's delicate gesture and is flooded with love and shame.

For now I have nothing more to say. I can't really get my thoughts together properly.

Annelise tells herself (every day!) that cleaning a stranger's house is almost exactly the same as cleaning her own. Is there really any difference between scrubbing the grime from someone else's bathtub and scouring the muck from her own? It requires the same circular motion, identical strength, and, for now, it's what she has to do for her family. So it's for the greater good. It's practically noble, she thinks with a laugh, on her knees, wiping sweat from her forehead with the back of her hand. Noble is not something she cares about.

In a schedule arranged by Mrs. Vogel through her network of local Jewish families, Annelise cleans for the Ashers on Mondays, the Wolfs on Tuesdays, and the Mandels on Thursdays. She takes the streetcar, drops Ruthie off at Lotte's on the way—and thank goodness for Lotte, who is always happy to watch her little girl.

Mrs. Wolf ignores her, which Annelise mostly appreciates, except that every Tuesday there is a note waiting for her on the kitchen table detailing all the things she did wrong the previous week. "Annelise, I noticed some streaks on the upstairs bathroom mirror last week. Perhaps I forgot to show you where we keep the vinegar. It's in the cupboard under the kitchen sink."

Mrs. Asher likes to clean *with* her, which jolts Annelise out of the reverie she tries to achieve, like an off-rhythm triangle

clanging in the middle of a concerto. Mrs. Asher follows her
around with a dust cloth wrapped around a broom, chirping
about the hard-to-reach corners of the house, the crevasses
only she understands to be in need of attention. Annelise
ignores her, pretending that she can't understand.

Mrs. Mandel is her favorite. She takes Annelise's coat when
she walks in the door and leaves her alone while she works.
She gives her lunch, baked chicken or an egg sandwich. She
feeds her without fanfare, with the understanding between
them that it is circumstance that places them where they
are—fate, not divine right. She treats Annelise not exactly as
an equal, but more like a niece.

Dr. and Mrs. Mandel have also provided an affidavit of support for her parents, so Annelise feels the gravitational pull of
gratitude and debt, a concoction that could almost be love.

"Come," Mrs. Mandel says to her on a very cold Thursday
morning in November, just as Annelise is wringing the dirty
mop into a bucket of dirtier gray water. Mrs. Mandel takes
the mop from her, touches Lise's cold hands. "Enough work
now. I'm making us hot cocoa. It's freezing in here!"

Lise follows Mrs. Mandel into the kitchen. There are two
blue china cups set on top of two pretty white saucers on
the table, and a green vase of fresh flowers between them.
The surfaces (thanks to Annelise) gleam. She feels as if she is
entering a still-life, sparkling with the fruits of her invisible
labors. A small pan of milk warms on the stove.

"Thank you," Annelise says, as Mrs. Mandel motions for her
to sit.

"We've talked about this, Lise," Mrs. Mandel says, lightly
chiding her. "You know you needn't thank me all the time!"

Annelise lightly traces the rim of her saucer. "I know. I'm sorry."

"Or apologize! You make *my* life so much easier," she says. Mrs. Mandel is in her fifties. Her children are grown, and her husband, the doctor, is gone all day. As far as Lise can tell, Mrs. Mandel mostly reads and knits and shops. Her life does seem quite easy.

Ruthie was up at dawn this morning, loud and cheerful as a robin ("Sun up!" she squawked at 5:20. "Ruthie up!"), and Walter, awakened by her shouts, sulked through breakfast, which was an ordeal. Now, finally sitting, Annelise feels a hard tug of exhaustion. She stifles a yawn.

Mrs. Mandel, facing the stove, says, "And your parents?" and Annelise wonders if she's lost the thread of the conversation.

"Not much news," she says. *Lise, do whatever you can, be more careful, don't make mistakes or they'll reject it, I know you're doing everything you can, do more.*

Outside the kitchen window, the sky is hard pewter. A squirrel dashes up to the bird feeder and terrorizes a sparrow.

She rests her head in her bleachy hands, just for a second, while Mrs. Mandel still has her back to Annelise, stirring. She is so tired.

"A little help, please!" her mother used to call from the kitchen when Annelise was younger. A little help drying dishes or setting the table or taking bread out of the oven or sweeping up after dinner. And Annelise, resentful, obedient, would wait a beat, and then go help.

Mrs. Mandel is saying something, and Annelise desperately hauls herself up from the muddy banks of her fatigue.

"Mmm," she says. She blinks hard and tries to sharpen her dull words. "I'm so sorry—I didn't hear you."

Mrs. Mandel turns, pot of cocoa in hand, and walks over to the table, pours a cup for Annelise and a cup for herself. "It's all right," she says. "Let's just sit together for a moment." She pulls out her chair. Passes Lise a cloth napkin. "I so enjoy your company."

Lise opens her mouth to say thank you, then closes it. Nods.

"We'll just sit here quietly," Mrs. Mandel says, "until it's time for you to get back to work."

What she misses:

Her mother and father, of course. The wrapped-in-a-cocoon feeling of being someone's child.

Is she still a daughter?

The corner of the dining room where she hid in the folds of a long pale curtain, waiting in a little dome of light for her mother to pretend not to know where she was.

Two silver candlesticks, delicate and filigreed and polished to a high gleam, rarely used.

Two brass candlesticks, heavy as bricks, used every Friday. She asked her mother once why they didn't use the pretty ones, but she can't remember her reply.

(All the replies she can't remember.)

Her cousin, Trude.

They were the same age, and so of course it was presumed they would play together, sleep in the same bed when the families visited, share their meals, share their days. But Trude and Annelise hated each other.

The earliest dispatch from the record of their mutual loathing was Trude's claim that Annelise had broken the neck of Gisela, her favorite doll. Annelise denied this tearfully, but in fact it was true. She snapped that doll's neck in a rage, because Trude had ripped seven pages out of her favorite book.

The story of their disdain would probably be apocryphal,

they might laugh about it over dinner, if they had been allowed to grow older together.

The pace of time unfolding.

Lying in bed, sick with the flu, sweating through her night-gown, miserable, the most miserable she had ever been, teeth chattering, thinking, *Am I dying?* Her mother, next to her, pressing a cold cloth to her forehead, giving her sips of water in a glass tumbler, whispering, *Drink a little bit, there, just a little bit.* The next day, a bowl of oatmeal and a slice of toast.

Her own language. The impossible ease of it.

Yellow morning light shining in through the bakery's front window. Lavender dusky light from the dining room window. The white-blue August afternoon sky. Miserable November 4:30 darkness falling. Her father, exhausted, silent at night. Her mother, overworked, grouchy, and sighing. Any of it. All of it.

What is the absence of fear? It's not courage. Is it boredom? Is it peace? It's been so long, she can't remember.

You write that we should go to Uncle Werner in France. That would be nice and good, but don't think that we can get our visas that quickly.

The few holidays Walter and Annelise enjoyed in Germany as a married couple were delightful excursions. They stayed in gracious hotels. She noted every detail on these trips—the way the curtains hung like thick, splendid tapestries, how the ornate silverware gleamed—so that she could describe them later to her mother and to Sofie. On their honeymoon, they went to Berlin and stayed at the Hotel Adlon on Unter den Linden, where the finery—the chandeliers and delicate linens, the marble floors and Oriental rugs—made her feel like a princess. *Ridiculous,* the practical side of her knew, but, just for four nights, she allowed herself to soak in the luxury as if it were a warm, lavender-scented bath. The next year, Walter left the store in Erich's increasingly capable hands, and they took the train and spent a weekend at a seaside resort in Sylt, where cool, salty air blew through the open windows of their hotel room, and they made love to the sound of waves crashing, slept for nine hours, and woke up starving. By the time Ruthie was born, in 1936, they were unwelcome in most establishments and too frightened to travel.

The first vacation they take in their new country is not what she expects. More specifically, since she has no idea what to expect, since every noun in this new language seems to have a slightly different meaning than it does in her native tongue, the holiday doesn't match her understanding of what a *holiday* is, or used to be.

"A *Sommerfrische*," Walter urged, against her protestations that they couldn't afford the trip. "I have one week off, and Ruthie has never breathed country air!" So, with the help of Walter's boss, they booked a week in a place called Three Lakes and invited Oskar and Charlotte, reserved adjoining cottages for the five of them—five and a half, because poor Charlotte is pregnant.

They find their cabin, confusingly named "Lazy Daze." Oskar and Charlotte's is called "Playin' Hooky," which is also incomprehensible to the group.

(Annelise and Charlotte are taking an English class that meets once a week in the basement of the library. Last week they learned idioms. *Barking up the wrong tree. Hit the hay. Let the cat out of the bag.* They and their nineteen fellow students are shy, tender things who share little but the embarrassment of not understanding the language they're steeped in. But the idioms sent them into gales of laughter. They forgot themselves. The teacher, a young woman, smiled at them sweetly, as if they were children.)

They walk through the door of the tiny cottage and are greeted by trapped heat and the smell of other people's vacations—cooking and babies and wet clothes, the lingering funk of damp crevasses. A dark-green welcome mat squishes disturbingly beneath Lise's open-toed summer shoes. She glances around the room and takes it all in: pine walls; a low tartan sofa; a brownish armchair; off to the side, a kitchenette; a stone fireplace, black with soot.

So, she thinks. *An American holiday.* Something different from the life they are living.

Her heart wants to see pleasure, but her eyes see grime. She understands that this will be a new kind of holiday, one that will involve scrubbing. But her habit in this country is not to complain; her habit is to deliberately and actively *not-complain,* to avoid grousing or protesting at all costs, and so she fixes a smile on her face, turns around to Walter and Oskar and Charlotte and Ruthie (who is wide-eyed, confused, index finger jammed in her mouth), and says, "Well, isn't this pleasant!" And Walter scoops Ruthie up into his arms and says, *"Yes!"* and Charlotte gives a little assenting chirp, and Oskar just laughs.

Later, after Oskar and Charlotte have gone to their own cottage to settle in, after Annelise and Walter have unpacked their bags and opened all of the windows, Walter takes Ruthie out for a walk on the beach. Annelise is alone. She trails her fingertips over the surfaces of the living room, surveys the little kitchen with her mother's gimlet eye—really just an oven and a few inches of countertop, an irregular alcove sliced out of the round living area like a hunk of cheese hacked from a truckle. She bends close to the stove and inhales deeply, shudders. She has never kept kosher, but there are some foods so wrong to her that they might as well be poison. She imagines a family: trim mother and hearty father, a girl with blond braids, freckled twin boys in caps. On warm nights, the children camp in sleeping bags on the porch. All this from the sniff of a stove! But there it is. The bacon of happy Gentiles.

There is a quick rap on the unlocked screen door, and

she straightens, takes four steps to where Oskar is standing politely, as if he can't see in, hands clasped behind his back.

"Charlotte is sleeping," he says. "And every time I move, I'm afraid I'm going to wake her up."

"Come in, please," Annelise says. "Sit down. I'll see if I can find some coffee." A slight breeze whiffles through the screen, makes its way halfway through the cottage and then gives up.

"Am I interrupting you?" he asks.

"Of course not." Annelise is flushed with pleasure at his unexpected visit. "Walter and Ruthie are out walking. I was just cleaning up a bit. Wondering about the people who stayed here before us."

"Charlotte found three dirty socks in our cottage and nearly collapsed."

She pauses. "Well, a three-footed man is a frightening thought." She feels giddy, suddenly, deserving. She's not sure of what.

"She had to lie down after that. For the baby. Charlotte believes all of the old wives' tales," Oskar says.

Annelise is digging through the small box of dry goods they'd brought with them, pulls out a small paper bag of coffee beans she ground at home.

"She eats an apple every day, so that the baby will have rosy cheeks."

"Well, no harm in that, hmm?" She fills a kettle of water and lights the stove.

"And she worries that if she's startled, the baby will be born with a birthmark. So I have to be very careful. Those dirty socks! Our poor little child is probably growing an enormous purple splotch on his back as we speak!"

Annelise lets out a loud and unexpected guffaw, and then Oskar is laughing, too, either at the ridiculousness of his own wife's superstitions, or at Lise's surprising (and, he'll admit, delightful) bark of laughter, and then there they are, the two of them, laughing so hard that Annelise has to sit down.

"Shhh," Oskar manages, gasping. "The walls are thin!"

Annelise recalls their apartment in Feldenheim, knocking on the wall behind her bed late at night to communicate with Max, when they were children, before he moved away: the rhythmic tapping of his perfect, comforting, meaningless replies.

"Oh!" Oskar whispers. "And she now cooks only the blandest meals, because, did you know, spicy foods can make the baby go *blind*!"

Oskar on the sofa and Annelise on the chair. They can't stop. They're looking at each other, crying with laughter.

And later, of course, Annelise will think, that first chortle was an innocent one, wasn't it? She did, for that brief moment, feel that she was laughing affectionately at Charlotte, the same way she is so charmed by Ruthie's childish confusion. But then they kept laughing, and it was no longer just that, if it ever really had been.

When they finish, finally, after Annelise has wiped her eyes with the corner of her sleeve and Oskar has stared at the ceiling for a few moments to collect himself, they look at each other again, and although neither has moved, the space between them has shrunk, and so Annelise, like a rabbit sensing danger, springs up to get the coffee.

She is pouring two cups when she hears Walter and Ruthie coming up the path, Walter's baritone and Ruthie's high chatter, and she quickly opens the cupboard and finds a third cup.

Ruthie walks in, coated in sand, head to foot, like a little cinnamon-dusted franzbrötchen. There is sand on her cheeks, in her dark hair. "Mama!" she announces, by way of greeting. "I want *you* to clean me up!" as if she were bestowing the greatest gift.

Annelise dashes over to her before Ruthie can loose sand all over the newly swept cottage, and Walter smiles at his wife, a fond mixture of apology and surrender.

Annelise bends and lifts Ruthie, carries her into the bathroom. Despite her efforts, sand rains from Ruthie's arms and legs as they walk, onto the floor, onto Annelise's arms, down the inside of her dress, irritating and inevitable.

"Oskar!" Walter says. "Hello!" And he lowers himself into the chair Annelise was sitting in just seconds ago.

You think, dear Lise, that we have been summoned to go to Stuttgart to the consulate and that we already have our visa. Unfortunately, you are very much mistaken. I was also wrong in writing that it could have been all arranged here in our town.

I haven't slept well for a number of nights. One bad thing comes after another.

Lise, you wanted to know what was wrong with me. Now I can tell you. I was ill for three months. I lost a tremendous amount of weight and was in the hospital for a week. I didn't think I would survive. These terrible times have left their mark on me.

But I am a bit better now. I'm seeing a Dr. Volkmann in Frankfurt. The first time I went, he didn't talk much. I think he didn't really like me!

During the day, they picnic on the beach or wander up and down the main street: a diner, a greengrocer, an ice cream parlor, a five-and-dime. Midday heat. Mosquitoes at sunset.

After dinner, Lise and Charlotte wash and dry the dishes. Lise puts Ruthie to bed. Then the four of them sit around the table and drink coffee, and because they've spent every moment of the day together, there is nothing much left to talk about, so, without discussion, Walter pulls out a deck of playing cards.

The *thwap* of the cards on the table is soothing. Nothing is required of them but the ability to organize and count, to tally numbers, maybe a little bit of strategy. The muted noise of their neighbors in nearby cabins is background music: dishes, laughter, the agitated rise and fall of overtired children. *It's not my fault! Give it back! She already had a turn!* Mothers at their wits' end. The occasional stern male voice. Children brought to order.

There are interludes of startling silence. Moths bounce against the screen door.

Still, after more than two years in America, Annelise is shocked to find herself in this purgatory of calm. Every day she tells herself that her life is real.

Yesterday she let herself walk barefoot along the edge of the water, her shoes and stockings yards away on the blanket.

The cold water lapped her feet—a combination of delight and pain she'd never felt before. She stayed there until her toes went numb.

And every night she's brought back to herself, turned inward to the fraying wire that connects her to her mother and father, attuned to a buzzing, metallic fear.

My dear ones, do whatever is in your power. I know it's not that easy, but you must try everything so that we can come to you quickly.

———

And the daytime calm she insists upon exposes itself, in the darkness, as fraud.

It's her turn to lay down a card. But she's drifted from the game, and it takes her a minute to return to the task, to reorganize her hand. Oskar, mid-sentence, is imitating an American accent that he could have gotten only from the movies: *"Okey dokey, partner."* Walter and Charlotte laugh. A few cabins away, a baby cries, then stops. Annelise takes a card from her hand without noticing what it is, lays it down on the pile.

Charlotte, four months along, has finally filled out, and now she is pleased to note that strangers glance at her belly and smile at her as if she looks like she is expecting rather than just suffering from a bout of stomach flu. She will not admit this to anyone, not even to Oskar, but she knows the exact moment this baby was conceived: Oskar on top of her, humming with pleasure, his face close to hers, fully present, the way he is only when they're making love, which is why she gives herself to him so often. This, she feels, is the power she has over him, the one pull she exerts. It's her secret calculation, a carnal mathematics. It's not that she minds it. It's just that part of what she enjoys is his weakness, her strength.

Their baby, their *child,* is due in December. In the crackling July heat, it seems an impossible world away. It feels to her as if it will never come. It's not the worst feeling to have.

Charlotte looks at Annelise's card and tries not to smile: the four of clubs, which she needs, and which, she thinks, means Annelise has stopped caring, because if her friend wants to, she can beat them at cards every night. She pretends to hesitate, then snaps it up, arranges her hand.

She watches her husband from behind her cards. He's feigning concentration, but he glances up to gaze around the table, looks at Annelise for just a moment longer than necessary. A blink, and Charlotte would have missed it. But she doesn't blink. She doesn't miss it. All right. She can wait until December. She can wait longer than any of them.

A mosquito whirs around the table and they take turns swatting at it, shooing it away from themselves and toward one another until Walter lets it alight on his arm and slaps it dead.

On their first day in Three Lakes, as they were settling into their cabin, Charlotte discovered the detritus of another family's recent stay there—a small, damp towel, a comb, and three dirty socks (*three*—where was the fourth? Was it lying in wait?)—and, after carefully picking them up and disposing of them, she became overwhelmed by the prospect of a solid week with her husband and her dear friends, the meals they would share and the endless conversations to which she would have to pay attention, and she told Oskar that she was exhausted and needed to lie down.

What she needed was privacy, the solace of quiet, her body's communion with itself. So she pulled the shades in the bedroom and lay down on the thin mattress on the creaky bedsprings and she rested her hands on her belly and calmed her mind. After a few minutes, she heard Oskar creep away and then, through the flimsy walls, she heard her husband and Annelise laughing, and her heart thudded with a quick and sickly dread. She thought that they were probably laughing at her. Then she convinced herself that they weren't. Either way: they might as well have been embracing. She lay still for a while, willing them to stop. The sound ringing through the walls was disembodied, ghastly.

She focused on her belly but felt nothing. The baby had not yet quickened. It was too early for that. "Oh!" she heard Annelise cry. *"Ohhhh!"*

She was so young when her father died. Twenty years old. He was sick, and then he was gone. She built scaffolding around herself: Oskar, Walter and Annelise, even little Ruthie, and now this baby, who would be a boy. She did exactly what she had to do.

They were still laughing. But after a few minutes, Charlotte realized she could slide right under that unpleasant music. She squeezed her eyes shut and let it slip over her and wisp away, and it became nothing to her.

For several days now I've put pen and paper at the ready in order to write to you, but I always hoped—in vain—to get a letter from you. Yesterday we got one dated the 7th of April, which of course was totally out of date, since we had already written to you and heard from you on May 20 and June 21. But since that time we haven't heard anything.

We have given up the apartment and moved into a smaller one. Our landlord promises we can keep the apartment until we emigrate, but I'm not sure that that's true. One nice day it may happen that he will change his mind, and then where would we go? Right now I'm not going to buy or do anything. We'll just wait and see what happens.

Oskar visits the occasion so often in his head, he sometimes forgets he wasn't actually there when it happened. His father, hurrying down a flight of stairs. Losing his footing, tripping, falling. Holding a box of tools. (Oskar was eleven years old. He found his father, splayed: hammer near his right shoulder, screwdriver behind his head.)

The stunning slide of one foot. The way it skidded out in front of him, his leg kicking straight. The crash of the box, the crack of his back against the twelfth and thirteenth steps, the smack of his head against the concrete floor. A dynamite blast of pain.

He dreams of his father's last thoughts. He dreams them, as if his father somehow gave Oskar his final moments. The leak in the roof that needs patching before it rains again. He must remember to tell Esther: move the chair, put a pot down, a towel, just in case. A flash of the children, as he tumbled through air: Lucie, so kind and quiet and observant, and Oskar, with his good, sharp mind. The lunch that was waiting for him in the kitchen, beef stew, potatoes. His grumbling stomach.

Life could just slam to a halt like that: the shock of the stumble, the fall.

———

In quiet moments, Lise lets herself into the apartment on Weinstrasse, her first home. The key wiggles into the lock, catches, and she's through the door. The hallway with the dim light and the narrow, fringed Oriental rug, scarlet and gold. Her mother's first words whenever she enters, even when she's grown, with a child of her own: *Hang up your coat, please!*

The particular smell of linen and wood polish and her mother's French bath soap, and yeast. The living room, messier than her mother would like it to be. Her cello and stand propped against the wall. Heavy white drapes. Sunday: the bakery is closed, so her father is in the armchair, reading; her mother is in the kitchen, bustling. The combination of objects and noises that defines a person forever. Her bedroom, east facing, dark in the afternoon, her unmade bed, a sweater on the floor. A little catch of anxiousness at what her mother will say. *The state of it, Annelise!*

One day, on the beach, she confesses it to Oskar, her habit of returning home. They're walking along the shore. Walter and Charlotte and Ruthie are up near the dunes, building a sand castle. She has a certain sense that Oskar will understand—not that she remembers her life in Germany with clarity, but that sometimes she is still there, a body at rest in her family's home. He's still trying to bring his mother and sister over, in an endless loop of paperwork and worry.

She tells him about how she moves through her old apartment, eyes closed, room to room. He nods but doesn't reply. She whispers the most shameful part of her confession: If she's there in her memory, who's to say she can't create a moment that's as true as life? Or even truer?

The lake's little waves roll and suck at the shore. Oskar stoops down to pick up an unusual stone. Annelise steps toward the water, then, gingerly, into it. Oskar follows, gasps. She tries not to look at his feet, for some reason. She gathers her summer skirt, he rolls his pants to the knees, and they wade in just a little farther. They stand, shoulder to shoulder.

"I don't think we'll be able to get them out," she says.

Yesterday we finally received the letter that we so desperately were hoping for, dated June 24, from which we were able to see that all of you are well. I, too, am a little better. Lise, the journey through Russia is known to us, too, and is the only one possible at the moment, but it is very difficult.

How do you imagine everything? You think it's so easy to leave. Order the tickets in August and travel in September? It used to be that way. We haven't heard a thing about our affidavit of support.

If only I could embrace all of you and hold you close to my heart. When will this happen?

It's the sorrow that follows them everywhere. It's inescapable, and it's the fuse of their connection; it *is* their connection. It's the two of them, alone in a damp room, their affection no compensation for all they have lost. Their attraction is sadness, is an attempt to fill the hole, is cold comfort, is comfort.

I do hope

Who knows whether we will even come, since it goes so terribly slowly. It could take at least another six years—something we can hardly imagine.

It is difficult for me to write this. When we were in Cologne, one of the gentlemen from the Aid Society told me that it would have to be noted in the affidavit that I am very ill. He said that I would consider myself very lucky if, under these circumstances, I could get the visa in Stuttgart.

I've accepted the fact that we cannot take any furniture along.

Be careful that you don't catch cold.

———

Years from now, when Annelise will be twice the age she is, she'll open the catalog in her mind and finally attempt to take inventory of what she lost. It will all be there: the teapots and the stubbed toes, the heat lightning and the tomatoes. The precise language of her world. Its humming sense of continuity (that pretty lie). The hard faces and the rock through the window and the typewriter. And all of the people she loved, every last one.

She'll be almost sixty years old before she'll muster up the iron will to do it, but she will. She'll fill in every outline. She'll etch every detail with a knife.

I have no strength left

I am terribly down. I'm afraid I will not recover.

About that letter

The handwriting is different, unfamiliar and recognizable at the same time. A scrawl, like a bird has skittered across the thin envelope, but legible. She is no fool. It's been coming for months. Look, it's been coming for years. She knows before she opens it. Her father has never written to her.

Here is where she is: in the kitchen, catching the best light of the day. She has hung a mirror above the sink to magnify the meager sunlight. There's a moment every day between breakfast and lunch when she sits at the little metal table and slowly sips a strong cup of coffee, the best moment. This is where she always is. She holds the letter, still possibly something else, continues to breathe, suspended in not-knowing.

Ruthie comes charging through the door from school, home for lunch. She takes up so much space, her beautiful girl. Annelise delights in the hot expanse of her daughter's body, the thickness of her legs, her pointy elbows cocked, her messy hair, her wild self. She is a force—alive, electrified, always starving.

"Mama!" she says. Annelise has often wondered how it is that they are all *Mama,* all of the women, the angry and the kind, the distracted and the attentive. It doesn't fit them all.

"Mama!" Ruthie is impatient if she's ignored, and Annelise knows she'll have to teach her restraint, better manners, but the truth is she thrills at this, too, at her little girl's demands for attention, her absolute insistence.

"Yes, my sweet," Annelise says, the letter still soft between her fingers.

"I am *hungry right now!*" Ruthie says, and stomps her foot, pretending to be mad, and smiles hugely up at Annelise.

The letter. The letter.

Annelise crouches down in front of her daughter, furrows her brow as if she's angry—a game they play; she is never ever truly angry. She's not built for it. "And what did I tell you about stomping your feet?" Annelise says, so close that she can see the flecks of black in Ruthie's dark-brown irises.

"You never told me anything about stomping my feet!" the little girl shouts, and, giggling, she jumps up and down and then flings herself into her mother's arms.

"How was your morning, little?"

"I pushed David on the swings. Mrs. Kahn told me my letters were marvelous, and they are marvelous! She read us a story and Nancy Bellamy talked out of turn in the middle of the story and she had to go sit in the hallway! I would never do that!"

She can wait until Ruthie goes back to school for the afternoon. She can wait until Walter comes home. She can wait until after dinner, can sit back down at the kitchen table at the end of the day, in her blue dressing gown, when this busy, useful room is finally dark, sponged down, swept clean, all of its duties dispatched.

She can wait until Ruthie graduates from high school. She

can wait until Ruthie meets a nice young man, gets married, has children. Yes, she can wait to open this letter until she herself is a grandmother.

Ruthie is quiet now, paging through a book while she waits for her lunch, humming to herself.

Annelise's heart squeezes.

She puts on an apron, tucks the envelope into its pocket. She feeds her daughter lunch.

Standing in front of the sink, she opens it.

May 31, 1941

My dear child,

Your dear mother has passed away. She suffered a great deal, and death was a relief for her. I have to find my own way now. I have dissolved our homestead in Feldenheim and now moved to Heldenbergen to be with your aunt Jenny. Since you know that I am not very good at writing letters, please accept just these few lines. My thoughts are always with you.

*Farewell and warmest greetings and
especially for our little Ruthie,
Your loving father*

I hope you can try something from your side so that I can get to you as quickly as possible.

———

Later, later she will howl. She'll sob into her pillow so that no one hears. She'll take some comfort in Walter's arms. For now, she folds the letter carefully and slips it back into its envelope. Ruthie spills a glass of milk, and Annelise swoops in with a cloth. "There," she says, and kisses Ruthie on the head, which smells a little sour, like sweat and grass and cheese. "Tonight is bath night," she says.

She will never see her mother again.

"Can I stay home with you today, Mama?" Ruthie asks, as she does every day.

Yes. "No, you have to go back to school. But you'll be home again before you know it."

"I'm all done eating." Ruthie pushes herself away from the table, slides down from her chair. Her plate is still half full. No matter. Sometimes Annelise eats Ruthie's half-finished lunch for her own. Not today. "Oh, I forgot to tell you," Ruthie says.

Annelise raises her eyebrows, nods.

"I learned how to hop today."

"Wonderful. Show me."

How strange, the convergences, darkness roaring into ordinary life.

Ruthie raises her right leg, bent at the knee, steadies herself. She begins with a tentative little jump, wobbles, bites her lip in concentration, quickly gains confidence. She hops around the kitchen.

Her mother is gone. Much later she will understand: murdered.

"Are you watching?" Ruthie is hopping in place now, panting a little.

"You're just like a bunny," Annelise says.

"Hop! Hop!" Ruthie hops to the edge of the kitchen and out into the hallway, thudding through the small apartment. "I'm in the bathroom now!" she calls.

The letter throbs in her pocket.

"Mama? I'm in the bathroom!"

"All right, Ruthie."

"I'm brushing my hair!"

"Good girl," she calls, clearing Ruthie's plate, her empty glass.

She will never see her mother again.

Ruthie narrates the details of her every move, feels the pressing need to tell her mother everything; in Annelise's reflection, Ruthie knows she exists. Annelise understands the impulse. "Good girl," she calls again.

She makes her way through the small apartment, toward the sound of her daughter's voice. She stands still outside the bathroom, arms outstretched, palms against opposite walls like a tree planted in the middle of the hallway. The soft fabric of her skirt skims her legs just below her knees. The dim hallway, the smell of the soup that she made this morning. Ruthie's high voice like a bird.

Annelise closes her eyes, heart pounding, blood rushing. Bones and breath.

She is mute with sorrow and filled with tenderness for this undeserving world.

Section Five

Clare dragged a wedge of blueberry pancake through a puddle of maple syrup. She and Matthew sat across from each other, so close she could see the faint creases at the corners of his eyes, the stubble on his chin.

They had been discussing a movie they were considering seeing that night. Was it getting good reviews? Should they maybe just stay in and order food? He was quiet for a minute, then looked down at his plate, stabbed a triangle of pancake with his fork, and gazed at it. "You should meet Jack," he said.

A little breeze blew in and rustled the newspapers on the counter. Her upstairs neighbors' cat scuttled overhead. Matthew was still gazing at his fork.

"Has Jack never met a pancake before?" she asked.

He looked up, half smiled at her, his teeth bluish. "Come home with me for a visit."

Clare paused, or froze: her entire body was alert to this sudden and particular moment, to the sticky amber syrup on their plates, the cooling coffee in her cup, music from a car on the street below Dopplering past, the pressure of the chair on the backs of her legs. She felt it all move through her, how they might look back on this exact moment years from now and think, "That was when it began," or, "That was when it died." Either was possible. They were right there, perched on that fault line.

She had spoken with Jack on the phone once, lying in Matthew's bed on a Saturday morning. He had a little-boy voice so high and sweet she felt a burst of ridiculous love, an oxytocin misfire, like a letter sent to the wrong address.

"Oh, hi!" he'd said to her. There was a slight echo on the line. "I'm actually drawing something!"

"How nice!" she said. "What is it?"

"I don't actually know yet. It's quite lovely, though. Could I talk to my dad, please?"

"So, what do you think?" Matthew asked her now. "Flights are cheap."

She speared another forkful of her pancake. The thought of leaving—even just the thought of it—was a seam coming loose. She felt the little stinging pop of it in her chest.

But he wasn't asking her to move to England with him. He was just asking her to meet his son. They could go on a Thursday, return on a Monday. She would return to work and her coworkers would hardly have missed her. "How was your weekend?" they would say. "Did ya have a good one?"

A visit to London. It was not a binding contract.

Still, she looked at Matthew and took quick note of the things that might annoy her—would! would definitely annoy her!—some day, in some possible future: the way he tapped his fingers incessantly on the edge of the table, how he extended his legs at an awkward angle so that anyone trying to navigate this little kitchen would just have to climb over them. He talked in his sleep. He could be pedantic. He was a back-seat driver even though he did not have his American driver's license and often got confused about which side of the road one was supposed to drive on.

It was a catalog of minor irritations, and she knew even as she was assembling it that it was no guarantee against future pain.

She chewed slowly, swallowed. "Okay," she said.

Matthew had stopped eating. He was just staring at her now, a dopey grin on his face.

"What?" Clare stood, embarrassed, hot. "What is it?"

"My two favorite people," he said.

She smiled as if she were someone who heard this kind of thing frequently, then gathered their dishes and took them to the sink. The forks clinked against each other; syrup stuck the plates together. She swiveled away from Matthew, turned the taps on and squirted green liquid soap onto a sponge.

"Why don't you leave the dishes for me?" Matthew said.

"It's all right. I don't mind."

terribly upset

How could she possibly go with him?

can't put into words

She was born to stay put.

"Right!" Matthew said, over the sound of the running water. "Then I'll start looking into flights!"

"Okay," she said again.

Why does she have to be so far away from us?

She was coiled in those words, trapped in their urgent, whispered pleas. They were like filaments wrapped around her chest, so beautiful she could hardly breathe.

*

They agreed to stay awake.

"It's better this way," Matthew insisted. He held Clare's

hand as he led her around his flat, which was narrow and recessed with little alcoves, like a rabbit warren. "I promise. If we can stay awake now, we'll sleep really well tonight, and then tomorrow our body clocks will have adjusted."

She couldn't quite understand what he was saying. She heard, "sleep" and "body clocks," and they stood in the doorway of his bedroom, its space taken up almost entirely by a big, fluffy cloud of a bed, and she felt a weariness so all-encompassing, she moaned softly. She tugged at his hand, tried to pull him toward the bed. He tugged back, laughing.

"Clare, I'm serious. Just wait a few more hours."

"How many?" she squeaked. Her throat was dry. Were these the first words she'd spoken since they'd walked into Matthew's apartment? His *flat*? Maybe. Yes.

He looked at his watch, grimaced. "Eight."

He made her a cup of tea and sat her down on the couch. "I'm going out for food," he said. "We need milk for a proper cup of tea. And bread and just a few other things. I'll be quick." He made her promise she wouldn't fall asleep.

She fell asleep as soon as the door clicked shut. She slept the dreamless death-sleep of the jet-lagged, and she woke to the sound of her own alarm clock in Milwaukee, although, as her head cleared to the noise, she thought it was strange that her alarm was buzzing when usually it jangled, and the light in her apartment seemed different, the feel of the pillow strangely scratchy against her cheek, and she wasn't in her apartment at all, and there was an odd little elf-woman standing over her, and a boy.

"Oh, God, I'm sorry," the elf said. She had very short white-blond hair and a tiny, pointy nose.

Clare sat up, blinked as the room swam, and then settled into focus. "Harf," she said, a combination of *Hello* and *who are you* and *elf.*

"Oh, I'm *so* sorry," the elf said again. "You're Clare, and you're exhausted. I'm Deirdre." She stuck out her hand and Clare stared at it. "We're a bit early. I am so sorry," the elf said again, and Clare remembered the day before, at the airport, as she and Matthew raced to their gate (late), how Matthew apologized to everyone he veered past, including, once, a metal pole: "Excuse me, I'm so sorry, sorry, pardon me."

And now the elf was saying, "This is Jack," and Clare finally snapped to—she was here, in Matthew's apartment in London, with, for some reason, his ex-wife and his son.

Jack looked up at her, skeptical. He wore small wire-framed glasses. His unkempt light brown hair stood up in tufts. It looked exactly like Matthew's in the morning. Clare cleared her throat and smiled at Deirdre and said to Jack, "Let's not tell your dad I was sleeping. I promised I would stay awake!" A flash of dismay sparked across Deirdre's pointy little face, and then Clare realized that she had just asked a four-year-old to lie to his father. "I'm just kidding! We'll tell your dad. We'll tell him as soon as he comes home that I fell asleep. We would never lie to your dad!" Jack sidled up closer to his mother and buried his face in her sleeve.

Matthew walked through the door, just in time, a cloth bag hanging from his arm. Jack disengaged from his mother and leapt at his father, and they both howled with delight. Clare glanced over at Deirdre, who had sat down on the other end of the couch and was gazing at Jack and Matthew with an inscrutable little smile.

How completely strange that she was witness to this intimate reunion, that these two particular humans had come together and made this little bespectacled creature, this person who wouldn't exist if Matthew's parents had decided to live somewhere else, if Deirdre had fallen for the bartender who'd asked for her number the week before she met Matthew, if Matthew had gone to a different university. What sheer cosmic oddity. This boy. These two people. This family! Clare swallowed a dry lump in her throat and felt like she was disappearing, which was probably just the jet lag.

Matthew lurched over to the couch, Jack suctioned around his torso, the sack of groceries still dangling from his wrist. "I picked up bread and milk and jam and this little jellyfish that just sort of attached itself to me. I was thinking we could have it for tea." Jack giggled, and Matthew kissed the top of his head.

Deirdre stood then and leaned toward her son and ex-husband, gave them a quick, encompassing hug. "Right," she said. "I'll be off. Have a good weekend," she said. "I'll pick you up on Monday, sweet. Remember to brush your teeth!"

"I will," Matthew said, and Jack melted into giggles again.

Clare had not pressed Matthew on the reasons for his divorce, and Matthew hadn't elaborated beyond a few sentences about marrying too young and growing apart. He said he thought Deirdre might be dating a woman now, but he didn't really have any evidence for it and anyway it didn't matter. He said it twice: *Anyway, it doesn't matter,* and so she put a check mark next to it in her brain, flagged it for later.

She knew now, watching them together, seeing the light pleasure they took in each other, the handing-off of their child, the no-nonsense hug, that in fact there was no simmering bitterness between them, no thwarted passion turned to resentment, and she was relieved. But the thickness in her throat remained. She missed her mother, suddenly, stupidly, like a foal on new legs. She had been in England for four hours. She was hot with homesickness.

They had two hours without Jack, late on Saturday afternoon. They dropped him at a birthday party around the corner in the midst of a rainstorm. ("Ah, Jack, love!" the birthday girl's mother said from the doorway, ushering the dripping child into her house. Then, to Matthew and Clare, with a wink: "Don't linger, you two! Off you go! Do not get sucked in!" She was sizing Clare up and cheerfully shooing them away at the same time. How did she do that?)

Nobody but Clare seemed to mind the pouring rain. "Lashing!" Matthew said. It came at them from above and also somehow sideways, swooshing up and around them. They were like pasta being rinsed in a colander.

Matthew pulled her closer under their utterly ineffective umbrella, which was about to turn inside out. They splashed up the street. The cobblestones under their feet were beautiful and slippery, like beach pebbles. Matthew steered them toward a doorway. "Come on. This is why we have pubs."

He held the door for her, shook out the umbrella on the front steps. The pub was warm and smelled of hops and wet wool. Matthew put his hand on her back and guided her to a table in the corner. All weekend, she had been led from place to place to place, thought to thought. She was still so tired, woozy with jet lag, almost feverish with it, and more malleable than usual. Matthew took her coat, and she sank into the booth. She liked the feeling, just for now—this sense of being wrapped in a blanket, of not having to make any decisions. Steam seemed to rise from her skin. She thought about her mother, at home in Milwaukee: running errands or telling her father a story about work or eating tomato soup, and she knew her mother was thinking about her.

"This is my fourth favorite pub!" Matthew said. He was so happy here, a lighter version of himself. And so, in a way she hadn't predicted, was she.

"My favorite," Matthew went on, "is called the Queen's Knickers."

Clare nodded sleepily, caught up in the warmth. She sipped the cider that had magically appeared in front of her. It took her a full minute to laugh.

At the bars her friends liked in Milwaukee, someone was always about to pinch your bottom or throw up next to you. This place, actually called the Windmill, was quiet, though there was one man at the bar slumped over and another, a few stools down, muttering to himself. Above the bar was a framed photograph of Princess Diana, who had died almost a year ago. In the picture, her hands were folded underneath her chin, and she was gazing off to the side benevolently.

Matthew took off his glasses and wiped them on his sleeve. "Clare," he said. "Thank you for doing this for me. With me. I'm so happy you're here." He leaned forward, unembarrassed. "I really am."

She slid a little lower in her seat and let out an assenting squeak.

My sweet Ruthie,

Today this letter is just for you, on your fourth birthday. I wish everything wonderful for you, my darling, everything I can imagine. Be a very good girl and listen to what your dear papa and your dear mama tell you, and you will become a fine girl. I know you will. I wish I could buy you a birthday present. Maybe your mama will get you a nice dress and she will say it's from me. That would be a present for both of us and would make me very happy. My sweetheart. Be healthy and good, and grow up big and strong, and for today let me give you a thousand greetings and a thousand kisses from your oma, who loves you more than anything in the world.

The day before they left, she'd had lunch with her mother. She took the bus to the bank downtown and met her in the cafeteria on the top floor. The room was huge, glass-windowed, drenched in light, and practically empty: Ruth liked a late lunch.

"We think there's a squirrel in the attic," her mother said as she forked a leaf of romaine. "Or mice. Oh, and raspberries are on sale at Zellman's. I know you love raspberries. Also did I tell you about Bob and Kiki Glaser's youngest daughter, Esmé?" Clare shook her head. "She moved to California and is now working as a character at Disneyland! Isn't that wild?" She held up a brownish lettuce leaf and scowled at it, deposited it on her napkin, then looked up at Clare. "Your eyebrows look nice!"

She talked and talked, barely pausing between subjects. The movie she and Mel had just seen. Her coworker Mary Jane, who believed that all ethnic cuisines were the same as Chinese, except Italian. The novel she was reading, the title and plot of which she couldn't recall at the moment. She was a high-octane version of herself. "Are you done packing? Do you have enough money for your trip?" Clare had finished her soup while her mother was still just stabbing at her salad, talking.

"I think you've killed it," Clare said, pointing at the salad. "I think it's dead now."

"Isn't this nice, though?" Ruth said finally. "Isn't it just so nice to be here together?" She set her fork down, ripped off a hunk of bread roll, put the smallest piece of it in her mouth, and just left it there for a moment, as if she'd forgotten how to chew.

A feeling floated between them, almost tangible. It was a thing they'd always known, a dark and lovely magic.

Could she break her mother's heart? That was the question. Then there would be shards between them, too.

"What's happening over there?" Matthew asked. He put his glasses back on. "What's going on in that head of yours?"

"Just thinking about the polar bears," Clare said. They'd started joking about it almost immediately after the dinner at her parents', insistently cementing their allegiance.

"Yes. Me, too. Always." Matthew nodded gravely.

Falling in love was a choreographed dance—of course it was! It was rhythmic and predictable, the most boring waltz. People met, they laughed at a joke, and then it became an inside joke. They shared a general sense of the world. They noted each other's food preferences, walked along a beach, and dipped their toes into icy water. They asked each other, "What's going on in that head of yours?"

But it was also this, right now, in a pub outside London: a jumble of timing and luck, lit by street lamps and driving rain, specific enough to convince her that this feeling could never, ever be replicated. She was sunk. She was gone.

Much later, she would remember her time with Jack as a series of Lego cities meticulously constructed, boisterously demolished.

There were other activities, of course—a trip to the museum, some hours in the park, the obligatory bus tour of the city—but her specific time with Jack was mostly a simple sequence of creation and destruction. All that was required of Clare was her participation. He would hand her a plastic block and tell her what to do with it, and she would oblige. Jack was watchful and serious. She didn't try to win him over, and he was not won over, but by the end of the weekend, they were friends, and when Deirdre came to pick him up on Monday morning, he was a person to her, someone she would miss.

She felt an inkling of how this might be, how she might slip into this domestic arrangement. For the first time in her life, she thought that she might be bigger than herself, that she might expand enough to fit inside someone else's life.

They were packing the last of their things. It was still rainy and gray outside, and their cab was due in two hours. Matthew was humming. She wanted to tell him. She wanted to say something about Jack, about how very glad she was to have started to know him. "I don't think I can do this," she said. She was as surprised as he was to hear those words!

Matthew held a neatly folded T-shirt in his hands. He froze.

"Oh, I can't." Her voice cracked. The sadness that snuck up on her the first morning—there it was again. No. It had been there the whole time. She couldn't compensate for it—the whole world of it in her veins.

"What can't you do?"

"You don't understand," she said. She had been gathering her things from the bathroom. Her hands were full now of tiny bottles. She was like a juggler who had suddenly, mid-show, lost her nerve. "I don't think . . . I'm just really connected to my parents. I can't live so far away from them." She started crying. She needed a tissue, but she didn't know what to do with the lotions and the creams. All of the little bottles.

"Clare." His face reddened. She watched as his posture changed, how he slumped a little as the wound spread. He unfolded the T-shirt he was holding, refolded it. "We haven't even . . . I thought we were . . ."

She dropped all of the little bottles into her suitcase, a shower of plastic, then swiped at her eyes with her sleeve.

"I thought you'd be willing to give it a go," he said. "And if it doesn't work, well, I mean, we could figure something else out."

She thought about the way Matthew took Jack's hand the second they walked out the door, how he cut up his food and asked him questions and listened to his answers. "How?" she said.

"I don't know! But it seems like you won't even entertain the idea. Like you don't even want to try. You're so sure you can't . . . just trust me?"

She liked him so much. He brought her coffee in the mornings and he read the books she recommended and then he asked her what she thought. He wanted to know everything about her. So what?

Her eyes blurred with tears. She was staring so intently at Matthew's face that his features took on an odd, surreal quality, as if they were slowly shifting from their usual spots, his nose skewing right, his eyes drifting apart, then together. He was the narcissistic med student, the noncommittal grad student, the sweet, boring computer guy. Then he was himself again, sharp and particular, brown eyes and small ears, smooth face, the little white scar on his forehead from when he was six and his sister threw a plate at him. He sat down heavily on the bed and leaned his head against the wall and Clare took in the curve of his neck, the arrangement of muscles and tendons and delicate bones.

"I can't just leave them. We don't . . . we don't do that in my family." He could never really understand the primordial soup from which she had emerged. She was obligation and reparation, rupture and remedy. She laughed out loud at the ridiculousness of it, the grandiosity! He lifted his head and looked at her, injured, and the gap between them filled with lava.

A tug of irritation worked at his mouth, pulled the corners down. She had never seen that before. "I am willing to try to figure this out with you, Clare," he said tightly. "But it can't be just me."

She closed her suitcase, snapped the clasp, and here she was again. Loneliness seeped through her, liquid and familiar. *If only I could see her.* It was the saddest she'd ever been, but it was also nothing at all.

*

They sat next to each other on the flight home and it wasn't as if they were strangers to each other, but they were like two people who'd had a one-night stand at a convention and were now quietly marinating in regret.

They were polite, murmuring apologies when one accidentally elbowed the other or brushed a cocktail napkin onto the floor. She wanted to tell Matthew: *You wouldn't believe this awkward situation I'm in!* and was felled by the fact that he was the situation.

He drove her home from the airport. He parked a block from her building and carried her suitcase for her and walked her to her door and kissed her. "I've a busy few days coming up," he said, and then he looked down at his feet, and she saw that he was as sad as she was. "I'll talk to you soon."

She sat for three days in the still aftermath of their unresolved argument and found it unbearable. If she broke up with him now, they would survive. Of course they would.

In her apartment she thumbed through Klara's letters, the originals. She ran her fingers lightly over the spiky script, the ancient crumbling edges.

Stay. Stay. It thudded inside her, indistinguishable from her own pulse.

She imagined herself in five years, in a house that looked like her parents' house but wasn't. There were babies everywhere! They squawked and yawped and crawled on the floor and wriggled about on the countertops, diapers dragging behind them like luggage. There was a fat one climbing a bookshelf, and a rangy one shimmying up a table leg. A dark-haired baby gummed the edge of the coffee table. A towheaded one sat in the middle of the floor, banging on a toy drum. A few floated near the ceiling, lazily hovering, shimmering strands of drool slowly falling from their pink mouths. One swung gleefully from a chandelier. There was one baby splashing in the bathroom sink, and another popping out of the toaster. Clare stood in the middle of the chaos, pregnant, turning in a slow circle. And there was her own mother, standing next to her, arms out. Arms out to the babies! Ruth bent low and scooped them up in twos and threes, murmured, "Come on, come here, it's all right, come." And the babies came to her, even the ones that were floating above. Those babies drifted down and landed, gently, in Ruth's outstretched, welcoming arms.

She finally walked over to Matthew's apartment with the thought of an end curling through her brain. It had rained earlier. It was bright now, but the warm air was still humid and heavy. She climbed up the steps to his building and wandered in through his open door. She made her way slowly across the living room, pulled her hands through her hair. He was subletting the apartment from a single, sixty-year-old professor on sabbatical in Belgium. The rooms were open and sunny, full of blond Ikea furniture, bright pillows and blankets and geometrically patterned rugs. They were the decorating vision of a lonely form of artificial intelligence.

She had practiced her speech on the way over. *This is not meant to be.*

She found Matthew in the kitchen, kneading dough. She watched for a moment as his arms worked, palms and fingers pressing. He was covered in flour—his hands, his cheek, the front of his blue T-shirt. She knew how to make bread, too. Rule number one: put on an apron.

"I was thinking about you," he said. "And I thought you might like to have some bread."

She felt it all, for one staggering second: love and terror, the only true equals.

Matthew stopped kneading, rested his hands lightly on the dough.

"Fun fact about me," he said. "I worked at a bakery when I was in school. I was fired for giving free biscuits to my friends."

Clare laughed. Light poured from him, golden.

She walked around to the other side of the kitchen counter and stood next to him, tucked her hands into her pockets. He swiped at his forehead and left another trail of flour there.

It would never be simple. One of them would always ache for home.

The smell of yeast rising was insistent, was ancestral comfort. It overrode her frontal lobe and stamped out logic. She was oxygen and confusion, unbearable weight and liftoff.

"I'm just so glad to see you," Matthew said.

The ghosts she traveled with gathered around them.

Clare nodded, didn't trust her voice. Grief like the tide behind her. Was this her fate? To be happy?

Matthew turned, bent to put the bread into the oven. Later he fed it to her, still steaming.

Children of immigrants are anthropologists of our own families. We're participant-observers of cultures we live in, but that will never quite belong to us.

I grew up in a suburb of Milwaukee in the 1970s and '80s. My maternal grandparents lived about ten minutes from us, and I spent a lot of time with them—family dinners every Friday and Sunday night, and visits almost every day after school. Their love was almost tangible: a heavy, warm blanket, freshly laundered and tucked around me a little bit too tightly.

In my memory, my grandparents bustle around my childhood, smelling of powder and wool, always present, always feeding me, kissing my head, praising my every accomplishment. (I believe I may have been the only child ever to tie her shoes so beautifully.)

They left Germany with my mother in 1938 and settled in Milwaukee. They spoke with such thick German accents that some of my friends thought they didn't speak English at all. They loved my brother and me so much that they never wanted us to leave the house: they preferred us close by, where they could keep their eyes on us—all of their eyes, all of the time. I remember staying over at their apartment for a night when my parents went out of town. Although they lived in a two-bedroom apartment, they set up cots for us in their bedroom—mine next to my grandmother's side of the bed, and my brother's next to my grandfather's, so they could keep watch over us through the night. I think I was eight or nine years old; my brother would have been ten or eleven—old enough, by most measures, to sleep in a room by ourselves!

There were silences in my family, questions I wanted to ask but was afraid to: about Germany, about what it had been like to leave, and about the people they'd left behind. But growing up in the shadow of trauma is about knowing, almost instinctively, what is too hot to touch.

I stood in their kitchen once, mustered up all of my courage, and asked them if they ever wanted to go back to Germany. I regretted the question as soon as the words were out of my mouth. They were both silent for a long few moments. My grandmother was standing at the stove, cooking, her back to me. She didn't turn around. She didn't say a word. My grandfather finally answered, softly: "No, *mein kind.*"

I was in my early twenties when I discovered the letters. In the last years of their lives, my grandparents had lived with us, and we kept the contents of their apartment in our basement. After they died, I found among their things a little wooden box full of letters written by my great-grandmother, Frieda, to my grandmother, Ilse, dating from 1938 to 1941. I knew almost immediately, and without being able to read a word, that this treasure I had stumbled upon would be life-changing. The letters were written in an old-fashioned German script that few people can still read. I was a graduate student in creative writing at the University of Minnesota at the time, and I found a German professor who was willing to help me. Every week, I would go to his office with a few of the letters and a little tape recorder, and he would read them to me, out loud, in English. It took us a year to translate all of them.

My great-grandmother's words felt like an introduction to her—her cadences were familiar, her love soaked with fear the source of the same concoction that was handed down to me. She was a woman trying to survive darkness, responding to it with ever increasing frenzy and barely contained despair. The letters weren't exactly specific. They didn't fill in all of the blanks my grandparents had left for me. They didn't tell me a coherent story about my family, exactly. They were more like a song, a howl of grief.

I knew right away that these letters were a gift, and that they were part of a story I wanted to tell. But it took me a very long time to figure out how to tell it. I wove them through a memoir that became my master's thesis, but I was only twenty-five, and memoir wasn't quite my format. I sat with them for another twenty years before I figured out (with the help of my agent, Julie Barer) that, in my hands, these letters were meant to inform a novel. I didn't know enough to tell my family's story as non-fiction. But I had enough information and enough imagination to tell this story, about a Jewish family in Germany on the edge of World War II, and about a young woman, fifty years later, in Milwaukee, trying to pry her own life apart from her history. And by this time I had daughters of my own, so I understood the heart of the story: the great, bottomless, complex, consuming love between mothers and daughters.

Send for Me is a novel. My great-grandmother's letters weave through it. The names are changed, but every word of the letters is true.

Acknowledgments

I have been living with this book for a long time, and I owe an enormous debt of gratitude to the many people who have supported me along the way. My profound thanks to Julie Barer and Jenny Jackson, the dream team. Thanks also to Nicole Cunningham, Maris Dyer, Amy Edelman, Maria Massey, and Abby Endler. Thank you to my friends and colleagues who read drafts of the book in its various forms, multiple times, and generously shared their thoughts: Erica Ackerberg, Rachel Baum, Liam Callanan, Christina Clancy, Carolyn Crooke, Christina Baker Kline, Elizabeth Larsen, Aims McGuinness, Jim Moore, Jon Olson, and Anuradha Rajurkar. Karl-Wilhelm Höffler, Peter Wyant, and Winson Chu offered invaluable genealogical and historical research and assistance. Professor Gerhard Weiss spent hours with me, many years ago, translating the letters that inspired this book. I'm grateful to him beyond measure, and I wish he were here to see the fruit of his efforts.

My gratitude to the GG Archives for allowing me to quote from their historical ship's brochures. I am also indebted to Marian A. Kaplan's *Between Dignity and Despair: Jewish Life in Nazi Germany* for providing me with invaluable background and insight into 1930s Germany.

Finally, I'm grateful to my family—my parents, whose love is the beating heart of this book; my daughters, who are my favorite humans and best companions; and my husband, Andrew Kincaid, whose unwavering love, support, and encouragement light the way.